"It Can't Be that You Want to Go Back to All
Those Society Shams, After You've Seen Real Life!"

I

INTO
THE PRIMITIVE

By ROBERT AMES BENNET

AUTHOR OF
"For the White Christ," "Thyra," Etc.

With Frontispiece in Colors
By ALLEN T. TRUE

To the man and to the beast;
To the girl, the snake, the blossom;
To fever and fire and fear;
To hurricane blast and storm within;
To bloody fang and venomed tooth;
To love, to hate, to pain, to joy,–
For of such is Life,
In the Primitive–and out.

CONTENTS

Into the Primitive

CHAPTER I

WAVE-TOSSED AND CASTAWAY

The beginning was at Cape Town, when Blake and Winthrope boarded the steamer as fellow passengers with Lady Bayrose and her party.

This was a week after Winthrope had arrived on the tramp steamer from India, and her Ladyship had explained to Miss Leslie that it was as well for her not to be too hasty in accepting his attentions. To be sure, he was an Englishman, his dress and manners were irreproachable, and he was in the prime of ripened youth. Yet Lady Bayrose was too conscientious a chaperon to be fully satisfied with her countryman's bare assertion that he was engaged on a diplomatic mission requiring reticence regarding his identity. She did not see why this should prevent him from confiding in *her*.

Notwithstanding this, Winthrope came aboard ship virtually as a member of her Ladyship's party. He was so quick, so thoughtful of her comfort, and paid so much more attention to her than to Miss Leslie, that her Ladyship had decided to tolerate him, even before Blake became a factor in the situation.

From the moment he crossed the gangway the American engineer entered upon a daily routine of drinking and gambling, varied only by attempts to strike up an off-hand acquaintance with Miss Leslie. This was Winthrope's opportunity, and his clever frustration of what Lady Bayrose termed "that low bounder's impudence" served to install him in the good graces of her Ladyship as well as in the favor of the American heiress.

Such, at least, was what Winthrope intimated to the persistent engineer with a superciliousness of tone and manner that would have stung even a British lackey to resentment. To Blake it was supremely galling. He could not rejoin in kind, and the slightest attempt at physical retort would have meant irons and confinement. It was a British ship. Behind Winthrope was Lady Bayrose; behind her Ladyship, as a matter of course, was all the despotic authority of the captain. In the circumstances, it was not surprising that the American drank heavier after each successive goading.

Meantime the ship, having touched at Port Natal, steamed on up the East Coast, into the Mozambique Channel.

On the day of the cyclone, Blake had withdrawn into his stateroom with a number of bottles, and throughout that fearful afternoon was blissfully unconscious of the danger. Even when the steamer went on the reef, he was only partially roused by the shock.

He took a long pull from a quart flask of whiskey, placed the flask with great care in his hip pocket, and lurched out through the open doorway. There he reeled headlong against the mate, who had rushed below with three of the crew to bring up Miss Leslie. The mate cursed him virulently, and in the same breath ordered two of the men to fetch him up on deck.

The sea was breaking over the steamer in torrents; but between waves Blake was dragged across to the side and flung over into the bottom of the one remaining boat. He served as a cushion to break the fall of Miss Leslie, who was tossed in after him. At the same time, Winthrope, frantic with fear, scrambled into the bows and cut loose. One of the sailors leaped, but fell short and went down within arm's length of Miss Leslie.

She and Winthrope saw the steamer slip from the reef and sink back into deep water, carrying down in the vortex the mate and the few remaining sailors. After that all was chaos to them. They were driven ashore before the terrific gusts of the cyclone, blinded by the stinging spoondrift to all else but the hell of breakers and coral reefs in whose midst they swirled so dizzily. And through it all Blake lay huddled on the bottom boards, gurgling blithely of spicy zephyrs and swaying hammocks.

There came the seemingly final moment when the boat went spinning stern over prow. . . . . .

Half sobered, Blake opened his eyes and stared solemnly about him. He was given little time to take his bearings. A smother of broken surf came seething up from one of the great breakers, to roll him over and scrape him a little farther up the muddy shore. There the flood deposited him for a moment, until it could gather force to sweep back and drag him down again toward the roaring sea that had cast him up.

Blake objected,—not to the danger of being drowned, but to interference with his repose. He had reached the obstinate stage. He grunted a protest. . . . . . Again the flood seethed up the shore, and rolled him away from the danger. This was too much! He set his jaw, turned over, and staggered to his feet. Instantly one of the terrific wind-blasts struck his broad back and sent him spinning for yards. He brought up in a shallow pool, beside a hummock.

Under the lee of the knoll lay Winthrope and Miss Leslie. Though conscious, both were draggled and bruised and beaten to exhaustion. They were together because they had come ashore together. When the boat capsized, Miss Leslie had been flung against the Englishman, and they had held fast to each other with the desperate clutch of drowning persons. Neither of them ever recalled how they gained the shelter of the hummock.

Blake, sitting waist-deep in the pool, blinked at them benignly with his pale blue eyes, and produced the quart flask, still a third full of whiskey.

"I shay, fren's," he observed, "ha' one on me. Won' cos' you shent—notta re' shent!"

"You fuddled lout!" shouted Winthrope. "Come out of that pool."

"Wassama'er pool! Pool's allri'!"

The Englishman squinted through the driving scud at the intoxicated man with an anxious frown. In all probability he felt no commiseration for the American; but it was no light matter to be flung up barehanded on the most unhealthful and savage stretch of the Mozambique coast, and Blake might be able to help them out of their predicament. To leave him in the pool was therefore not to be thought of. So soon as he had drained his bottle, he would lie down, and that would be the end of him. As any attempt to move him forcibly was out of the question, the situation demanded that Winthrope justify his intimations of diplomatic training. After considering the problem for several minutes, he met it in a way that proved he was at least not lacking in shrewdness and tact.

"See here, Blake," he called, in another lull between the shrieking gusts, "the lady is fatigued. You're too much of a gentleman to ask her to come over there."

It required some moments for this to penetrate Blake's fuddled brain. After a futile attempt to gain his feet, he crawled out of the pool on all fours, and, with tears in his eyes, pressed his flask upon Miss Leslie. She shrank away from him, shuddering, and drew herself up in a huddle of flaccid limbs and limp garments. Winthrope, however, not only accepted the flask, but came near to draining it.

Blake squinted at the diminished contents, hesitated, and cast a glance of maudlin gallantry at Miss Leslie. She lay coiled, closer than before, in a draggled heap. Her posture suggested sleep. Blake stared at her, the flask extended waveringly before him. Then he brought it to his lips, and drained out the last drop.

"Time turn in," he mumbled, and sprawled full length in the brackish ooze. Immediately he fell into a drunken stupor.

Winthrope, invigorated by the liquor, rose to his knees, and peered around. It was impossible to face the scud and spoondrift from the furious sea; but to leeward he caught a glimpse of a marsh flooded with salt water, its reedy vegetation beaten flat by the storm. He himself was beaten down by a terrific gust. Panting and trembling, he waited for the wind to lull, in hope that he might obtain a clearer view of his surroundings. Before he again dared rise to his feet, darkness swept down with tropical suddenness and blurred out everything.

The effect of the whiskey soon passed, and Winthrope huddled between his companions, drenched and exhausted. Though he could hear Miss Leslie moaning, he was too miserable himself to inquire whether he could do anything for her.

Presently he became aware that the wind was falling. The centre of the cyclone had passed before the ship struck, and they were now in the outermost circle of the vast whirlwind. With the consciousness of this change for the better, Winthrope's fear-racked nerves relaxed, and he fell into a heavy sleep.

CHAPTER II

WORSE THAN WILDERNESS

A wail from Miss Leslie roused the Englishman out of a dream in which he had been swimming for life across a sea of boiling oil. He sat up and gazed about him, half dazed. The cyclone had been followed by a dead calm, and the sun, already well above the horizon, was blazing upon them over the glassy surfaces of the dying swells with fierce heat.

Winthrope felt about for his hat. It had been blown off when, at the striking of the steamer, he had rushed up on deck. As he remembered, he straightened, and looked at his companions. Blake lay snoring where he had first outstretched himself, sleeping the sleep of the just—and of the drunkard. The girl, however, was already awake. She sat with her hands clasped in her lap, while the tears rolled slowly down her cheeks.

"My—ah—dear Miss Genevieve, what is the matter?" exclaimed Winthrope.

"Matter? Do you ask, when we are here on this wretched coast, and may not get away for weeks? Oh, I did so count on the London season this year! Lady Bayrose promised that I should be among those presented."

"Well, I—ah—fancy, Lady Bayrose will do no more presenting—unless it may be to the heavenly choir, you know."

"Why, what do you mean, Mr. Winthrope? You told me that she and the maids had been put in the largest boat—"

"My dear Miss Genevieve, you must remember that I am a diplomat. It was all quite sufficiently harrowing, I assure you. They were, indeed, put into the largest boat—Beastly muddle!—While they waited for the mate to fetch you, the boat was crushed alongside, and all in it drowned."

"Drowned!—drowned! Oh, dear Lady Bayrose! And she'd travelled so much—oh, oh, it is horrible! Why did she persuade me to visit the Cape? It was only to be with her—And then for us to start off for India, when we might have sailed straight to England! Oh, it is horrible! horrible! And my maid, and all—It cannot be possible!"

"Pray, do not excite yourself, my dear Miss Genevieve. Their troubles are all over. Er—Gawd has taken them to Him, you know."

"But the pity of it! To be drowned—so far from home!"

13

"Ah, if that's all you're worrying about!—I must say I'd like to know how we'll get a snack for breakfast. I'm hungry as a—er—groom."

"Eating! How can you think of eating, Mr. Winthrope—and all the others drowned? This sun is becoming dreadfully hot. It is unbearable! Can you not put up some kind of an awning?"

"Well, now, I must say, I was never much of a hand at such things, and really I can't imagine what one could rig up. There might have been a bit of sail in the boat, but one can't see a sign of it. I fancy it was smashed."

Miss Leslie ventured a glance at Blake. Though still lying as he had sprawled in his drunkenness, there was a comforting suggestion of power in his broad shoulders and square jaw.

"Is he still—in that condition?"

"Must have slept it off by this time, and there's no more in the flask," answered Winthrope. Reaching over with his foot, he pushed against Blake's back.

"Huh! All right," grunted the sleeper, and sat up, as had Winthrope, half dazed. Then he stared around him, and rose to his feet. "Well, what in hell! Say, this is damn cheerful!"

"I fancy we are in a nasty fix. But I say, my man, there is a woman present, and your language, you know—"

Blake turned and fixed the Englishman with a cold stare.

"Look here, you bloomin' lud," he said, "there's just one thing you're going to understand, right here and now. I'm not your man, and we're not going to have any of that kind of blatter. Any fool can see we're in a tight hole, and we're like to keep company for a while— probably long as we last."

"What—ah—may I ask, do you mean by that?"

Blake laughed harshly, and pointed from the reef-strewn sea to the vast stretches of desolate marsh. Far inland, across miles of brackish lagoons and reedy mud-flats, could be seen groups of scrubby, half-leafless trees; ten or twelve miles to the southward a rocky headland jutted out into the water; otherwise there was nothing in sight but sea and swamp. If it could not properly be termed a sea-view, it was at least a very wet landscape.

"Fine prospect," remarked Blake, dryly. "We'll be in luck if the fever don't get the last of us inside a month; and as for you two, you'd have as much show of lasting a month as a toad with a rattlesnake, if it wasn't for Tom Blake,—that's my name—Tom Blake,—and as long as this shindy lasts, you're welcome to call me Tom or Blake, whichever suits.

But understand, we're not going to have any more of your bloody, bloomin' English condescension. Aboard ship you had the drop on me, and could pile on dog till the cows came home. Here I'm Blake, and you're Winthrope."

"Believe me, Mr. Blake, I quite appreciate the—ah—situation. And now, I fancy that, instead of wasting time—"

"It's about time you introduced me to the lady," interrupted Blake, and he stared at them half defiantly, yet with a twinkle in his eyes.

Miss Leslie flushed. Winthrope swore softly, and bit his lip. Aboard ship, backed by Lady Bayrose and the captain, he had goaded the American at pleasure. Now, however, the situation was reversed. Both title and authority had been swept away by the storm, and he was left to shift for himself against the man who had every reason to hate him for his overbearing insolence. Worse still, both he and Miss Leslie were now dependent upon the American, in all probability for life itself. It was a bitter pill and hard to swallow.

Blake was not slow to observe the Englishman's hesitancy. He grinned.

"Every dog has his day, and I guess this is mine," he said. "Take your time, if it comes hard. I can imagine it's a pretty stiff dose for your ludship. But why in—why in frozen hades an American lady should object to an introduction to a countryman who's going to do his level best to save her pretty little self from the hyenas—well, it beats me."

Winthrope flushed redder than the girl.

"Miss Leslie, Mr. Blake," he murmured, hoping to put an end to the situation.

But yet Blake persisted. He bowed, openly exultant.

"You see, Miss," he said, "I know the correct thing quite as much as your swells. I knew all along you were Jenny Leslie. I ran a survey for your dear papa when he was manipulating the Q. T. Railroad, and he did me out of my pay."

"Oh, but Mr. Blake, I am sure it must be a mistake; I am sure that if it is explained to papa—"

"Yes; we'll cable papa to-night. Meantime, we've something else to do. Suppose you two get a hustle on yourselves, and scrape up something to eat. I'm going out to see what's left of that blamed old tub."

"Surely you'll not venture to swim out so far!" protested Winthrope. "I saw the steamer sink as we cast off."

"Looks like a mast sticking up out there. Maybe some of the rigging is loose."

"But the sharks! These waters swarm with the vile creatures. You must not risk your life!"

"'Cause why? If I do, the babes in the woods will be left without even the robins to cover them, poor things! But cheer up!—maybe the mud-hens will do it with lovely water-lilies."

"Please, Mr. Blake, do not be so cruel!" sobbed Miss Leslie, her tears starting afresh. "The sun makes my head ache dreadfully, and I have no hat or shade, and I'm becoming so thirsty!"

"And you think you've only to wait, and half a dozen stewards will come running with parasols and ice water. Neither you nor Winthrope seem to 've got your eyes open. Just suppose you get busy and do something. Winthrope, chase yourself over the mud, and get together a mess of fish that are not too dead. Must be dozens, after the blow. As for you, Miss Jenny, I guess you can pick up some reeds, and rig a headgear out of this handkerchief— Wait a moment. Put on my coat, if you don't want to be broiled alive through the holes of that peek-a-boo."

"But I say, Blake—" began Winthrope.

"Don't say—do!" rejoined Blake; and he started down the muddy shore.

Though the tide was at flood, there was now no cyclone to drive the sea above the beach, and Blake walked a quarter of a mile before he reached the water's edge. There was little surf, and he paused only a few moments to peer out across the low swells before he commenced to strip.

Winthrope and Miss Leslie had been watching his movements; now the girl rose in a little flurry of haste, and set to gathering reeds. Winthrope would have spoken, but, seeing her embarrassment, smiled to himself, and began strolling about in search of fish.

It was no difficult search. The marshy ground was strewn with dead sea-creatures, many of which were already shrivelling and drying in the sun. Some of the fish had a familiar look, and Winthrope turned them over with the tip of his shoe. He even went so far as to stoop to pick up a large mullet; but shrank back, repulsed by its stiffness and the unnatural shape into which the sun was warping it.

He found himself near the beach, and stood for half an hour or more watching the black dot far out in the water,—all that was to be seen of Blake. The American, after wading off-shore another quarter of

16

a mile, had reached swimming depth, and was heading out among the reefs with steady, vigorous strokes. Half a mile or so beyond him Winthrope could now make out the goal for which he was aiming,—the one remaining topmast of the steamer.

"By Jove, these waters are full of sharks!" murmured Winthrope, staring at the steadily receding dot until it disappeared behind the wall of surf which spumed up over one of the outer reefs.

A call from Miss Leslie interrupted his watch, and he hastened to rejoin her. After several failures, she had contrived to knot Blake's handkerchief to three or four reeds in the form of a little sunshade. Her shoulders were protected by Blake's coat. It made a heavy wrap, but it shut out the blistering sun-rays, which, as Blake had foreseen, had quickly begun to burn the girl's delicate skin through her open-work bodice.

Thus protected, she was fairly safe from the sun. But the sun was by no means the worst feature of the situation. While Winthrope was yet several yards distant, the girl began to complain to him. "I'm so thirsty, Mr. Winthrope! Where is there any water? Please get me a drink at once, Mr. Winthrope!"

"But, my dear Miss Leslie, there is no water. These pools are all sea-water. I must say, I'm deuced dry myself. I can't see why that cad should go off and leave us like this, when we need him most."

"Indeed, it is a shame—Oh, I'm so thirsty! Do you think it would help if we ate something?"

"Make it all the worse. Besides, how could we cook anything? All these reeds are green, or at least water-soaked."

"But Mr, Blake said to gather some fish. Had you not best—"

"He can pick up all he wants. I shall not touch the beastly things."

"Then I suppose there is nothing to do but wait for him."

"Yes, if the sharks do not get him."

Miss Leslie uttered a little moan, and Winthrope, seeing that she was on the verge of tears, hastened to reassure her. "Don't worry about him, Miss Genevieve! He'll soon return, with nothing worse than a blistered back. Fellows of that sort are born to hang, you know."

"But if he should be—if anything should happen to him!"

Winthrope shrugged his shoulders, and drew out his silver cigarette case. It was more than half full, and he was highly gratified to find that neither the cigarettes nor the vesta matches in the cover had been reached by the wet.

"By Jove, here's luck!" he exclaimed, and he bowed to Miss Leslie. "Pardon me, but if you have no objections—"

The girl nodded as a matter of form, and Winthrope hastened to light the cigarette already in his fingers. The smoke by no means tended to lessen the dryness of his mouth; yet it put him in a reflective mood, and in thinking over what he had read of shipwrecked parties, he remembered that a pebble held in the mouth is supposed to ease one's thirst.

To be sure, there was not a sign of a pebble within miles of where they sat; but after some reflection, it occurred to him that one of his steel keys might do as well. At first Miss Leslie was reluctant to try the experiment, and only the increasing dryness of her mouth forced her to seek the promised relief. Though it failed to quench her thirst, she was agreeably surprised to find that the little flat bar of metal eased her craving to a marked degree.

Winthrope now thought to rig a shade as Miss Leslie had done, out of reeds and his handkerchief, for the sun was scorching his unprotected head. Thus sheltered, the two crouched as comfortably as they could upon the half-dried crest of the hummock, and waited impatiently for the return of Blake.

CHAPTER III

THE WORTH OF FIRE

Though the sea within the reefs was fast smoothing to a glassy plain in the dead calm, they did not see Blake on his return until he struck shallow water and stood up to wade ashore. The tide had begun to ebb before he started landward, and though he was a powerful swimmer, the long pull against the current had so tired him that when he took to wading he moved at a tortoise-like gait.

"The bloomin' loafer!" commented Winthrope. He glanced quickly about, and at sight of Miss Leslie's arching brows, hastened to add: "Beg pardon! He–ah–reminds me so much of a navvy, you know."

Miss Leslie made no reply.

At last Blake was out of the water and toiling up the muddy beach to the spot where he had left his clothes. While dressing he seemed to recover from his exertions in the water, for the moment he had finished, he sprang to his feet and came forward at a brisk pace.

As he approached, Winthrope waved his fifth cigarette at him with languid enthusiasm, and called out as heartily as his dry lips would permit: "I say, Blake, deuced glad the sharks didn't get you!"

"Sharks?–bah! All you have to do is to splash a little, and they haul off."

"How about the steamer, Mr. Blake?" asked Miss Leslie, turning to face him.

"All under but the maintopmast–curse it!–wire rigging at that! Couldn't even get a bolt."

"A bolt?"

"Not a bolt; and here we are as good as naked on this infernal– Hey, you! what you doing with that match? Light your cigarette–light it!– Damnation!"

Heedless of Blake's warning cry, Winthrope had struck his last vesta, and now, angry and bewildered, he stood staring while the little taper burned itself out. With an oath, Blake sprang to catch it as it dropped from between Winthrope's fingers. But he was too far away. It fell among the damp rushes, spluttered, and flared out.

For a moment Blake knelt, staring at the rushes as though stupefied; then he sprang up before Winthrope, his bronzed face purple with anger.

"Where's your matchbox? Got any more?" he demanded.

"Last one, I fancy—yes; last one, and there are still two cigarettes. But look here, Blake, I can't tolerate your talking so deucedly—"

"You idiot! you—you— Hell! and every one for cigarettes!"

From a growl Blake's voice burst into a roar of fury, and he sprang upon Winthrope like a wild beast. His hands closed upon the Englishman's throat, and he began to shake him about, paying no heed to the blows his victim showered upon his face and body, blows which soon began to lessen in force.

Terror-stricken, Miss Leslie put her hands over her eyes, and began to scream—the piercing shriek that will unnerve the strongest man. Blake paused as though transfixed, and as the half-suffocated Englishman struggled in his grasp, he flung him on the ground, and turned to the screaming girl.

"Stop that squawking!" he said. The girl cowed down. "So; that's better. Next time keep your mouth shut."

"You—you brute!"

"Good! You've got a little spunk, eh?"

"You coward—to attack a man not half your strength!"

"Steady, steady, young lady! I'm warm enough yet; I've still half a mind to wring his fool neck."

"But why should you be so angry! What has he done, that you—"

"Why—why? Lord! what hasn't he done! This coast fairly swarms with beasts. We've not the smell of a gun; and now this idiot—this dough-head—has gone and thrown away our only chance—fire—and on his measly cigarettes!" Blake choked with returning rage.

Winthrope, still panting for breath, began to creep away, at the same time unclasping a small penknife. He was white with fear; but his gray eyes—which on shipboard Blake had never seen other than offensively supercilious—now glinted in a manner that served to alter the American's mood.

"That'll do," he said. "Come here and show me that knife."

"I'll show it you where it will do the most good," muttered Winthrope, rising hastily to repel the expected attack.

"So you've got a little sand, too," said Blake, almost good-naturedly. "Say, that's not so bad. We'll call it quits on the matches. Though how you could go and throw them away—"

"Deuce take it, man! How should I know? I've never before been in a wreck."

"Neither have I—this kind. But I tell you, we've got to keep our think tanks going. It's a guess if we see to-morrow, and that's no joke. Now do you wonder I got hot?"

"Indeed, no! I've been an ass, and here's my hand to it—if you really mean it's quits."

"It's quits all right, long as you don't run out of sand," responded Blake, and he gripped the other's soft hand until the Englishman winced. "So; that's settled. I've got a hot temper, but I don't hold grudges. Now, where're your fish?"

"I—well, they were all spoiled."

"Spoiled?"

"The sun had shrivelled them."

"And you call that spoiled! We're like to eat them rotten before we're through with this picnic. How about the pools?"

"Pools? Do you know, Blake, I never thought of the pools. I stopped to watch you, and then we were so anxious about you—"

Blake grunted, and turned on his heel to wade into the half-drained pool in whose midst he had been deposited by the hurricane.

Two or three small fish lay faintly wriggling on the surface. As Blake splashed through the water to seize them, his foot struck against a living body which floundered violently and flashed a brilliant forked tail above the muddy water. Blake sprang over the fish, which was entangled in the reeds, and with a kick, flung it clear out upon the ground.

"A coryphene!" cried Winthrope, and he ran forward to stare at the gorgeously colored prize.

"Coryphene?" repeated Blake, following his example. "Good to eat?"

"Fine as salmon. This is only a small one, but—"

"Fifteen pounds, if an ounce!" cried Blake, and he thrust his hand in his pocket. There was a moment's silence, and Winthrope, glancing up, saw the other staring in blank dismay.

"What's up!" he asked.

"Lost my knife."

"When?—in the pool? If we felt about—"

"No; aboard ship, or in the surf—"

"Here is my knife."

"Yes; almost big enough to whittle a match! Mine would have done us some good."

"It is the best steel."

21

"All right; let's see you cut up the fish."

"But you know, Blake, I shouldn't know how to go about it. I never did such a thing."

"And you, Miss Jenny? Girls are supposed to know about cooking."

"I never cooked anything in all my life, Mr. Blake, and it's alive,–and–and I am very thirsty, Mr. Blake!"

"Lord!" commented Blake. "Give me that knife."

Though the blade was so small, the American's hand was strong. After some little haggling, the coryphene was killed and dressed. Blake washed both it and his hands in the pool, and began to cut slices of flesh from the fish's tail.

"We have no fire," Winthrope reminded him, flushing at the word.

"That's true," assented Blake, in a cheerful tone, and he offered Winthrope two of the pieces of raw flesh. "Here's your breakfast. The trimmed piece is for Miss Leslie."

"But it's raw! Really, I could not think of eating raw fish. Could you, Miss Leslie?"

Miss Leslie shuddered. "Oh, no!–and I'm so thirsty I could not eat anything."

"You bet you can!" replied Blake. "Both of you take that fish, and go to chewing. It's the stuff to ease your thirst while we look for water. Good Lord!–in a week you'll be glad to eat raw snake. Finnicky over clean fish, when you swallow canvas-back all but raw, and beef running blood, and raw oysters with their stomachs full of disintegrated animal matter, to put it politely! You couldn't tell rattlesnake broth from chicken, and dog makes first-rate veal–when you've got to eat it. I've had it straight from them that know, that over in France they eat snails and fish-worms. It's all a matter of custom or the style."

"To be sure, the Japanese eat raw fish," admitted Winthrope.

"Yes; and you'd swallow your share of it if you had an invite to a swell dinner in Tokio. Go on now, both of you. It's no joke, I tell you. You've got to eat, if you expect to get to water before night. Understand? See that headland south? Well, it's a hundred to one we'll not find water short of there, and if we make it by night, we'll be doing better than I figure from the look of these bogs. Now go to chewing. That's it! That's fine, Miss Jenny!"

Miss Leslie had forced herself to take a nibble of the raw fish. The flavor proved less repulsive than she had expected, and its moisture was

22

so grateful to her parched mouth that she began to eat with eagerness. Not to be outdone, Winthrope promptly followed her lead. Blake had already cut himself a second slice. After he had cut more for his companions, he began to look them over with a closeness that proved embarrassing to Miss Leslie.

"Here's more of the good stuff," he said. "While you're chewing it, we'll sort of take stock. Everybody shell out everything. Here's my outfit—three shillings, half a dozen poker chips, and not another blessed— Say, what's become of that whiskey flask? Have you seen my flask?"

"Here it is, right beside me, Mr. Blake," answered Miss Leslie. "But it is empty."

"Might be worse! What you got?—hair-pins, watch? No pocket, I suppose?"

"None; and no watch. Even most of my pins are gone," replied the girl, and she raised her hand to her loosely coiled hair.

"Well, hold on to what you've got left. They may come in for fish-hooks. Let's see your shoes."

Miss Leslie slowly thrust a slender little foot just beyond the hem of her draggled white skirt.

"Good Lord!" groaned Blake, "slippers, and high heels at that! How do you expect to walk in those things?"

"I can at least try," replied the girl, with spirit.

"Hobble! Pass 'em over here, Winnie, my boy."

The slippers were handed over. Blake took one after the other, and wrenched off the heel close to its base.

"Now you've at least got a pair of slippers," he said, tossing them back to their owner. "Tie them on tight with a couple of your ribbons, if you don't want to lose them in the mud. Now, Winthrope, what you got beside the knife?"

Winthrope held out a bunch of long flat keys and his cigarette case. He opened the latter, and was about to throw away the two remaining cigarettes when Blake grasped his wrist.

"Hold on! even they may come in for something. We'll at least keep them until we need the case."

"And the keys!"

"Make arrow-heads, if we can get fire."

"I've heard of savages making fire by rubbing wood."

"Yes; and we're a long way from being savages,—at present. All the show we have is to find some kind of quartz or flint, and the sooner we start to look the better. Got your slippers tied, Miss Jenny?"

"Yes; I think they'll do."

"Think! It's knowing's the thing. Here, let me look."

The girl shrank back; but Blake stooped and examined first one slipper and then the other. The ribbons about both were tied in dainty bows. Blake jerked them loose and twisted them firmly over and under the slippers and about the girl's slender ankles before knotting the ends.

"There; that's more like. You're not going to a dance," he growled.

He thrust the empty whiskey flask into his hip pocket, and went back to pass a sling of reeds through the gills of the coryphene.

"All ready now," he called. "Let's get a move on. Keep my coat closer about your shoulders, Miss Jenny, and keep your shade up, if you don't want a sunstroke."

"Thank you, Blake, I'll see to that," said Winthrope. "I'm going to help Miss Leslie along. I've fastened our two shades together, so that they will answer for both of us."

"How about yourself, Mr. Blake?" inquired the girl. "Do you not find the sun fearfully hot?"

"Sure; but I wet my head in the sea, and here's another souse."

As he rose with dripping head from beside the pool, he slung the coryphene on his back, and started off without further words.

CHAPTER IV

A JOURNEY IN DESOLATION

Morning was well advanced, and the sun beat down upon the three with almost overpowering fierceness. The heat would have rendered their thirst unendurable had not Blake hacked off for them bit after bit of the moist coryphene flesh.

In a temperate climate, ten miles over firm ground is a pleasant walk for one accustomed to the exercise. Quite a different matter is ten miles across mud-flats, covered with a tangle of reeds and rushes, and frequently dipping into salt marsh and ooze. Before they had gone a mile Miss Leslie would have lost her slippers had it not been for Blake's forethought in tying them so securely. Within a little more than three miles the girl's strength began to fail.

"Oh, Blake," called Winthrope, for the American was some yards in the lead, "pull up a bit on that knoll. We'll have to rest a while, I fancy. Miss Leslie is about pegged."

"What's that?" demanded Blake. "We're not half-way yet!"

Winthrope did not reply. It was all he could do to drag the girl up on the hummock. She sank, half-fainting, upon the dry reeds, and he sat down beside her to protect her with the shade. Blake stared at the miles of swampy flats which yet lay between them and the out-jutting headland of gray rock. The base of the cliff was screened by a belt of trees; but the nearest clump of green did not look more than a mile nearer than the headland.

"Hell!" muttered Blake, despondently. "Not even a short four miles. Mush and sassiety girls!"

Though he spoke to himself, the others heard him. Miss Leslie flushed, and would have risen had not Winthrope put his hand on her arm.

"Could you not go on, and bring back a flask of water for Miss Leslie?" he asked. "By that time she will be rested."

"No; I don't fetch back any flasks of water. She's going when I go, or you can come on to suit yourselves."

"Mr. Blake, you—you won't go, and leave me here! If you have a sister—if your mother—"

"She died of drink, and both my sisters did worse."

"My God, man! do you mean to say you'll abandon a helpless young girl?"

"Not a bit more helpless than were my sisters when you rich folks' guardians of law and order jugged me for the winter, 'cause I didn't have a job, and turned both girls into the street—onto the street, if you know what that means—one only sixteen and the other seventeen. Talk about helpless young girls— Damnation!"

Miss Leslie cringed back as though she had been struck. Blake, however, seemed to have vented his anger in the curse, for when he again spoke, there was nothing more than impatience in his tone. "Come on, now; get aboard. Winthrope couldn't lug you a half-mile, and long's it's the only way, don't be all day about it. Here, Winthrope, look to the fish."

"But, my dear fellow, I don't quite take your idea, nor does Miss Leslie, I fancy," ventured Winthrope.

"Well, we've got to get to water, or die; and as the lady can't walk, she's going on my back. It's a case of have-to."

"No! I am not—I am not! I'd sooner die!"

"I'm afraid you'll find that easy enough, later on, Miss Jenny. Stand by, Winthrope, to help her up. Do you hear? Take the knife and fish, and lend a hand."

There was a note in Blake's voice that neither Winthrope nor Miss Leslie dared disregard. Though scarlet with mortification, she permitted herself to be taken pick-a-back upon Blake's broad shoulders, and meekly obeyed his command to clasp her hands about his throat. Yet even at that moment, such are the inconsistencies of human nature, she could not but admire the ease with which he rose under her weight.

Now that he no longer had the slow pace of the girl to consider, he advanced at his natural gait, the quick, tireless stride of an American railroad-surveyor. His feet, trained to swamp travel in Louisiana and Panama, seemed to find the firmest ground as by instinct, and whether on the half-dried mud of the hummocks or in the ankle-deep water of the bogs, they felt their way without slip or stumble.

Winthrope, though burdened only with the half-eaten coryphene, toiled along behind, greatly troubled by the mud and the tangled reeds, and now and then flung down by some unlucky misstep. His modish suit, already much damaged by the salt water, was soon smeared afresh with a coating of greenish slime. His one consolation was that Blake, after jeering at his first tumble, paid no more attention to him. On the other hand, he was cut by the seeming indifference of Miss Leslie. Intent on his own misery, he failed to consider that the girl might be suffering far greater discomfort and humiliation.

26

More than three miles had been covered before Blake stopped on a hummock. Releasing Miss Leslie, he stretched out on the dry crest of the knoll, and called for a slice of the fish. At his urging, the others took a few mouthfuls, although their throats were now so parched that even the moist flesh afforded scant relief. Fortunately for them all, Blake had been thoroughly trained to endure thirst. He rested less than ten minutes; then, taking Miss Leslie up again like a rag doll, he swung away at a good pace.

The trees were less than half a mile distant when he halted for the second time. He would have gone to them without a pause though his muscles were quivering with exhaustion, had not Miss Leslie chanced to look around and discover that Winthrope was no longer following them. For the last mile he had been lagging farther and farther behind, and now he had suddenly disappeared. At the girl's dismayed exclamation, Blake released his hold, and she found herself standing in a foot or more of mud and water. The sweat was streaming down Blake's face. As he turned around, he wiped it off with his shirtsleeves.

"Do you—can it be, Mr. Blake, that he has had a sunstroke?" asked Miss Leslie.

"Sunstroke? No; he's just laid down, that's all. I thought he had more sand—confound him!"

"But the sun is so dreadfully hot, and I have his shade."

"And he's been tumbling into every other pool. No; it's not the sun. I've half a mind to let him lie—the paper-legged swell! It would no more than square our aboard-ship accounts."

"Surely, you would not do that, Mr. Blake! It may be that he has hurt himself in falling."

"In this mud?—bah! But I guess I'm in for the pack-mule stunt all around. Now, now; don't yowl, Miss Jenny. I'm going. But you can't expect me to love the snob."

As he splashed away on the return trail, Miss Leslie dabbed at her eyes to check the starting tears.

"Oh, dear—Oh, dear!" she moaned; "what have I done, to be so treated? Such a brute, Oh, dear!—and I am so thirsty!"

In her despair she would have sunk down where she stood had not the sliminess of the water repelled her. She gazed longingly at the trees, in the fore of which stood a grove of stately palms. The half-mile seemed an insuperable distance, but the ride on Blake's back had rested her, and thirst goaded her forward.

Stumbling and slipping, she waded on across the inundated ground, and came out upon a half-baked mud-flat, where the walking was much easier. But the sun was now almost directly overhead, and between her thirst and the heat, she soon found herself faltering. She tottered on a few steps farther, and then stopped, utterly spent As she sank upon the dried rushes, she glanced around, and was vaguely conscious of a strange, double-headed figure following her path across the marsh. All about her became black.

The next she knew, Blake was splashing her head and face with brackish water out of the whiskey flask. She raised her hand to shield her face, and sat up, sick and dizzy.

"That's it!" said Blake. He spoke in a kindly tone, though his voice was harsh and broken with thirst. "You're all right now. Pull yourself together, and we'll get to the trees in a jiffy."

"Mr. Winthrope—?"

"I'm here, Miss Genevieve. It was only a wrenched ankle. If I had a stick, Blake, I fancy I could make a go of it over this drier ground."

"And lay yourself up for a month. Come, Miss Jenny, brace up for another try. It's only a quarter-mile, and I've got to pack him."

The girl was gasping with thirst; yet she made an effort, and assisted by Blake managed to gain her feet. She was still dizzy; but as Blake swung Winthrope upon his back, he told her to take hold of his arm. Winthrope held the shade over her head. Thus assisted, and sheltered from the direct beat of the sun-rays, she tottered along beside Blake, half unconscious.

Fortunately the remaining distance lay across a stretch of bare dry ground, for even Blake had all but reached the limit of endurance. Step by step he labored on, staggering under the weight of the Englishman, and gasping with a thirst which his exertions rendered even greater than that of his companions. But through the trees and brush which stretched away inland in a wall of verdure he had caught glimpses of a broad stream, and the hope of fresh water called out every ounce of his reserve strength.

At last the nearest palm was only a few paces distant. Blake clutched Miss Leslie's arm, and dragged her forward with a rush, in a final outburst of energy. A moment later all three lay gasping in the shade. But the river was yet another hundred yards distant. Blake waited only to regain his breath; then he staggered up and went on. The others, unable to rise, gazed after him in silent misery.

Soon Blake found himself rushing through the jungle along a broad trail pitted with enormous footprints; but he was so near mad with thirst that he paid no heed to the spoor other than to curse the holes for the trouble they gave him. Suddenly the trail turned to the left and sloped down a low bank into the river. Blind to all else, Blake ran down the slope, and dropping upon his knees, plunged his head into the water.

At first his throat was so dry that he could no more than rinse his mouth. With the first swallow, his swollen tongue mocked him with the salt, bitter taste of sea-water. The tide was flowing! He rose, sputtering and choking and gasping. He stared around. There was no question that he was on the bank of a river and would be certain of fresh water with the ebb tide. But could he endure the agony of his thirst all those hours?

He thought of his companions.

"Good God!" he groaned, "they're goners anyway!"

He stared dully up the river at the thousands of waterfowl which lined its banks. Within close view were herons and black ibises, geese, pelicans, flamingoes, and a dozen other species of birds of which he did not know the names. But he sat as though in a stupor, and did not move even when one of the driftwood logs on a mud-shoal a few yards up-stream opened an enormous mouth and displayed two rows of hooked fangs. It was otherwise when the noontime stillness was broken by a violent splashing and loud snortings down-stream. He glanced about, and saw six or eight monstrous heads drifting towards him with the tide.

"What in— Whee! a whole herd of hippos!" he muttered. "That's what the holes mean."

The foremost hippopotamus was headed directly for him. He glared at the huge head with sullen resentment. For all his stupor, he perceived at once that the beast intended to land; and he sat in the middle of its accustomed path. His first impulse was to spring up and yell at the creature. Then he remembered hearing that a white hunter had recently been killed by these beasts on one of the South African lakes. Instead of leaping up, he sank down almost flat, and crawled back around the turn in the path. Once certain that he was hidden from the beasts, he rose to his feet and hastened back through the jungle.

He was almost in view of the spot where he had left Winthrope and Miss Leslie, when he stopped and stood hesitating.

"I can't do it," he muttered; "I can't tell her,—poor girl!"

He turned and pushed into the thicket. Forcing a way through the tangle of thorny shrubs and creepers, until several yards from the path, he began to edge towards the face of the jungle, that he might peer out at his companions, unseen by them.

There was more of the thicket before him than he had thought, and he was still fighting his way through it, when he was brought to a stand by a peculiar cry that might have been the bleat of a young lamb: "Ba–ba!"

"What's that!" he croaked.

He stood listening, and in a moment he again heard the cry, this time more distinctly: "Blak!–Blak!"

There could be no mistake. It was Winthrope calling for him, and calling with a clearness of voice that would have been physically impossible half an hour since. Blake's sunken eyes lighted with hope. He burst through the last screen of jungle, and stared towards the palm under which he had left his companions. They were not there.

Another call from Winthrope directed his gaze more seaward. The two were seated beside a fallen palm, and Miss Leslie had a large round object raised to her lips. Winthrope was waving to him.

"Cocoanuts!" he yelled. "Come on!"

Three of the palms had been overthrown by the hurricane, and when Blake came up, he found the ground strewn with nuts. He seized the first he came to; but Winthrope held out one already opened. He snatched it from him, and placed the hole to his swollen lips. Never had champagne tasted half so delicious as that cocoanut milk. Before he could drain the last of it through the little opening, Winthrope had the husks torn from the ends of two other nuts, and the convenient germinal spots gouged open with his penknife.

Blake emptied the third before he spoke. Even then his voice was hoarse and strained. "How'd you strike 'em?"

"I couldn't help it," explained Winthrope. "Hardly had you disappeared when I noticed the tops of the fallen palms, and thought of the nuts. There was one in the grass not twenty feet from where we lay."

"Lucky for you–and for me, too, I guess," said Blake. "We were all three down for the count. But this settles the first round in our favor. How do you like the picnic, Miss Jenny?"

"Miss Leslie, if you please," replied the girl, with hauteur.

"Oh, say, Miss Jenny!" protested Blake, genially. "We live in the same boarding-house now. Why not be folksy? You're free to call me

Tom. Pass me another nut, Winthrope. Thanks! By the way, what's your front name? Saw it aboard ship–Cyril–"

"Cecil," corrected Winthrope, in a low tone.

"Cecil–Lord Cecil, eh?–or is it only The Honorable Cecil?"

"My dear sir, I have intimated before that, for reasons of–er–State–"

"Oh, yes; you're travelling incog., in the secret service. Sort of detective–"

"Detective!" echoed Winthrope, in a peculiar tone.

Blake grinned. "Well, it is rawther a nawsty business for your honorable ludship. But there's nothing like calling things by their right names."

"Right names–er–I don't quite take you. I have told you distinctly, my name is Cecil Winthrope!"

"O-h-h! how lovely!–See-sill! See-seal!–Bet they called you Sissy at school. English, chum of mine told me your schools are corkers for nicknames. What'll we make it–Sis or Sissy?"

"I prefer my patronymic, Mr. Blake," replied Winthrope.

"All right, then; we'll make it Pat, if that's your choice. I say, Pat, this juice is the stuff for wetness, but it makes a fellow remember his grub. Where'd you leave that fish?"

"Really, I can't just say, but it must have been where I wrenched my ankle."

"You cawn't just say! And what are we going to eat?"

"Here are the cocoanuts."

"Bright boy! go to the head of the class! Just take some more husk off those empty ones."

Winthrope caught up one of the nuts, and with the aid of his knife, stripped it of its husk. At a gesture from Blake, he laid it on the bare ground, and the American burst it open with a blow of his heel. It was an immature nut, and the meat proved to be little thicker than clotted cream. Blake divided it into three parts, handing Miss Leslie the cleanest.

Though his companions began with more restraint, they finished their shares with equal gusto. Winthrope needed no further orders to return to his husking. One after another, the nuts were cracked and divided among the three, until even Blake could not swallow another mouthful of the luscious cream.

Toward the end Miss Leslie had become drowsy. At Winthrope's urging, she now lay down for a nap, Blake's coat serving as a pillow. She

31

fell asleep while Winthrope was yet arranging it for her. Blake had turned his back on her, and was staring moodily at the hippopotamus trail, when Winthrope hobbled around and sat down on the palm trunk beside him.

"I say, Blake," he suggested, "I feel deuced fagged myself. Why not all take a nap?"

"'And when they awoke, they were all dead men,'" remarked Blake.

"By Jove, that sounds like a joke," protested the Englishman. "Don't rag me now."

"Joke!" repeated Blake. "Why, that's Scripture, Pat, Scripture! Anyway, you'd think it no joke to wake up and find yourself going down the throat of a hippo."

"Hippo?"

"Dozens of them over in the river. Shouldn't wonder if they've all landed, and 're tracking me down by this time."

"But hippopotami are not carnivorous—they're not at all dangerous, unless one wounds them, out in the water."

"That may be; but I'm not taking chances. They've got mouths like sperm whales—I saw one take a yawn. Another thing, that bayou is chuck full of alligators, and a fellow down on the Rand told me they're like the Central American gavials for keenness to nip a swimmer."

"They will not come out on this dry land."

"Suppose they won't—there're no other animals in Africa but sheep, eh?"

"What can we do? The captain told me that there are both lions and leopards on this coast."

"Nice place for them, too, around these trees," added Blake. "Lucky for us, they're night-birds mostly,—if that Rand fellow didn't lie. He was a Boer, so I guess he ought to know."

"To be sure. It's a nasty fix we're in for to-night. Could we not build some kind of a barricade?"

"With a penknife! Guess we'll roost in a tree."

"But cannot leopards climb? It seems to me that I have heard—"

"How about lions?"

"They cannot; I'm sure of that."

"Then we'll chance the leopards. Just stretch out here, and nurse that ankle of yours. I don't want to be lugging you all year. I'm going to hunt a likely tree."

CHAPTER V

THE RE-ASCENT OF MAN

Afternoon was far advanced, and Winthrope was beginning to feel anxious, when at last Blake pushed out from among the close thickets. As he approached, he swung an unshapely club of green wood, pausing every few paces to test its weight and balance on a bush or knob of dirt.

"By Jove!" called Winthrope; "that's not half bad! You look as if you could bowl over an ox."

Blake showed that he was flattered.

"Oh, I don't know," he responded; "the thing's blamed unhandy. Just the same, I guess we'll be ready for callers to-night."

"How's that?"

"Show you later, Pat, me b'y. Now trot out some nuts. We'll feed before we move camp."

"Miss Leslie is still sleeping."

"Time, then, to roust her out. Hey, Miss Jenny, turn out! Time to chew."

Miss Leslie sat up and gazed around in bewilderment.

"It's all right, Miss Genevieve," reassured Winthrope. "Blake has found a safe place for the night, and he wishes us to eat before we leave here."

"Save lugging the grub," added Blake. "Get busy, Pat."

As Winthrope caught up a nut, the girl began to arrange her disordered hair and dress with the deft and graceful movements of a woman thoroughly trained in the art of self-adornment. There was admiration in Blake's deep eyes as he watched her dainty preening. She was not a beautiful girl—at present she could hardly be termed pretty; yet even in her draggled, muddy dress she retained all the subtle charms of culture which appeal so strongly to a man. Blake was subdued. His feelings even carried him so far as an attempt at formal politeness, when they had finished their meal.

"Now, Miss Leslie," he began, "it's little more than half an hour to sundown; so, if you please, if you're quite ready, we'd best be starting."

"Is it far?"

"Not so very. But we've got to chase through the jungle. Are you sure you're quite ready?"

"Quite, thank you. But how about Mr. Winthrope's ankle?"

33

"He'll ride as far as the trees. I can't squeeze through with him, though."

"I shall walk all the way," put in Winthrope.

"No, you won't. Climb aboard," replied Blake, and catching up his club, he stooped for Winthrope to mount his back. As he rose with his burden, Miss Leslie caught sight of his coat, which still lay in a roll beside the palm trunk.

"How about your coat, Mr. Blake?" she asked. "Should you not put it on?"

"No; I'm loaded now. Have to ask you to look after it. You may need it before morning, anyway. If the dews here are like those in Central America, they are d-darned liable to bring on malarial fever."

Nothing more was said until they had crossed the open space between the palms and the belt of jungle along the river. At other times Winthrope and Miss Leslie might have been interested in the towering screw-palms, festooned to the top with climbers, and in the huge ferns which they could see beneath the mangroves, in the swampy ground on their left. Now, however, they were far too concerned with the question of how they should penetrate the dense tangle of thorny brush and creepers which rose before them like a green wall. Even Blake hesitated as he released Winthrope, and looked at Miss Leslie's costume. Her white skirt was of stout duck; but the flimsy material of her waist was ill-suited for rough usage.

"Better put the coat on, unless you want to come out on the other side in full evening dress," he said. "There's no use kicking; but I wish you'd happened to have on some sort of a jacket when we got spilled."

"Is there no path through the thicket?" inquired Winthrope.

"Only the hippo trail, and it don't go our way. We've got to run our own line. Here's a stick for your game ankle."

Winthrope took the half-green branch which Blake broke from the nearest tree, and turned to assist Miss Leslie with the coat. The garment was of such coarse cloth that as Winthrope drew the collar close about her throat Miss Leslie could not forego a little grimace of repugnance. The crease between Blake's eyes deepened, and the girl hastened to utter an explanatory exclamation: "Not so tight, Mr. Winthrope, please! It scratches my neck."

"You'd find those thorns a whole lot worse," muttered Blake.

"To be sure; and Miss Leslie fully appreciates your kindness," interposed Winthrope.

"I do indeed, Mr. Blake! I'm sure I never could go through here without your coat."

"That's all right. Got the handkerchief?"

"I put it in one of the pockets."

"It'll do to tie up your hair."

Miss Leslie took the suggestion, knotting the big square of linen over her fluffy brown hair.

Blake waited only for her to draw out the kerchief, before he began to force a way through the jungle. Now and then he beat at the tangled vegetation with his club. Though he held to the line by which he had left the thicket, yet all his efforts failed to open an easy passage for the others. Many of the thorny branches sprang back into place behind him, and as Miss Leslie, who was the first to follow, sought to thrust them aside, the thorns pierced her delicate skin, until her hands were covered with blood. Nor did Winthrope, stumbling and hobbling behind her, fare any better. Twice he tripped headlong into the brush, scratching his arms and face.

Blake took his own punishment as a matter of course, though his tougher and thicker skin made his injuries less painful. He advanced steadily along the line of bent and broken twigs that marked his outward passage, until the thicket opened on a strip of grassy ground beneath a wild fig-tree.

"By Jove!" exclaimed Winthrope, "a banyan!"

"Banyan? Well, if that's British for a daisy, you've hit it," responded Blake. "Just take a squint up here. How's that for a roost?"

Winthrope and Miss Leslie stared up dubiously at the edge of a bed of reeds gathered in the hollow of one of the huge flattened branches at its junction with the main trunk of the banyan, twenty feet above them.

"Will not the mosquitoes pester us, here among the trees?" objected Winthrope.

"Storm must have blown 'em away. I haven't seen any yet."

"There will be millions after sunset."

"Maybe; but I bet they keep below our roost"

"But how are we to get up so high?" inquired Miss Leslie.

"I can swarm this drop root, and I've a creeper ready for you two," explained Blake.

Suiting action to words, he climbed up the small trunk of the air root, and swung over into the hollow where he had piled the reeds. Across the broad limb dangled a rope-like creeper, one end of which he had fastened to a branch higher up. He flung down the free end to Winthrope.

"Look lively, Pat," he called. "The sun's most gone, and the twilight don't last all night in these parts. Get the line around Miss Leslie, and do what you can on a boost."

"I see; but, you know, the vine is too stiff to tie."

Blake stifled an oath, and jerked the end of the creeper up into his hand. When he threw it down again, it was looped around and fastened in a bowline knot.

"Now, Miss Leslie, get aboard, and we'll have you up in a jiffy," he said.

"Are you sure you can lift me?" asked the girl, as Winthrope slipped the loop over her shoulders.

Blake laughed down at them. "Well, I guess yes! Once hoisted a fellow out of a fifty-foot prospect hole—big fat Dutchman at that. You don't weigh over a hundred and twenty."

He had stretched out across the broadest part of the branch. As Miss Leslie seated herself in the loop, he reached down and began to haul up on the creeper, hand over hand. Though frightened by the novel manner of ascent, the girl clung tightly to the line above her head, and Blake had no difficulty in raising her until she swung directly beneath him. Here, however, he found himself in a quandary. The girl seemed as helpless as a child, and he was lying flat. How could he lift her above the level of the branch?

"Take hold the other line," he said. The girl hesitated. "Do you hear? Grab it quick, and pull up hard, if you don't want a tumble!"

The girl seized the part of the creeper which was fastened above, and drew herself up with convulsive energy. Instantly Blake rose to his knees, and grasping the taut creeper with one hand, reached down with the other, to swing the girl up beside him on the branch.

"All right, Miss Jenny," he reassured her as he felt her tremble. "Sorry to scare you, but I couldn't have made it without. Now, if you'll just hold down my legs, we'll soon hoist his ludship."

He had seated her in the broadest part of the shallow hollow, where the branch joined the main trunk of the fig. Heaped with the reeds which he had gathered during the afternoon, it made such a cozy shelter that she at once forgot her dizziness and fright. Nestling among the reeds, she leaned over and pressed down on his ankles with all her strength.

36

The loose end of the creeper had fallen to the ground when Blake lifted her upon the branch, and Winthrope was already slipping into the loop. Blake ordered him to take it off, and send up the club. As the creeper was again flung down, a black shadow swept over the jungle.

"Hello! Sunset!" called Blake. "Look sharp, there!"

"All ready," responded Winthrope.

Blake drew in a full breath, and began to hoist. The position was an awkward one, and Winthrope weighed thirty or forty pounds more than Miss Leslie. But as the Englishman came within reach of the descending loop, he grasped it and did what he could to ease Blake's efforts. A few moments found him as high above the ground as Blake could raise him. Without waiting for orders, he swung himself upon the upper part of the creeper, and climbed the last few feet unaided. Blake grunted with satisfaction as he pulled him in upon the branch.

"You may do, after all," he said. "At any rate, we're all aboard for the night; and none too soon. Hear that!"

"What?"

"Lion, I guess—Not that yelping. Listen!"

The brief twilight was already fading into the darkness of a moonless night, and as the three crouched together in their shallow nest, they were soon made audibly aware of the savage nature of their surroundings. With the gathering night the jungle wakened into full life. From all sides came the harsh squawking of birds, the weird cries of monkeys and other small creatures, the crash of heavy animals moving through the jungle, and above all the yelp and howl and roar of beasts of prey.

After some contention with Winthrope, Blake conceded that the roars of his lion might be nothing worse than the snorting of the hippopotami as they came out to browse for the night. In this, however, there was small comfort, since Winthrope presently reasserted his belief in the climbing ability of leopards, and expressed his opinion that, whether or not there were lions in the neighborhood, certain of the barking roars they could hear came from the throats of the spotted climbers. Even Blake's hair bristled as his imagination pictured one of the great cats creeping upon them in the darkness from the far end of their nest limb, or leaping down out of the upper branches.

The nerves of all three were at their highest tension when a dark form swept past through the air within a yard of their faces. Miss Leslie uttered a stifled scream, and Blake brandished his club. But Winthrope, who had caught a glimpse of the creature's shape, broke into a nervous laugh.

"It's only a fruit bat," he explained. "They feed on the banyan figs, you know."

In the reaction from this false alarm, both men relaxed, and began to yield to the effects of the tramp across the mud-flats. Arranging the reeds as best they could, they stretched out on either side of Miss Leslie, and fell asleep in the middle of an argument on how the prospective leopard was most likely to attack.

Miss Leslie remained awake for two or three hours longer. Naturally she was more nervous than her companions, and she had been refreshed by her afternoon's nap. Her nervousness was not entirely due to the wild beasts. Though Blake had taken pains to secure himself and his companions in loops of the creeper, fastened to the branch above, Winthrope moved about so restlessly in his sleep that the girl feared he would roll from the hollow.

At last her limbs became so cramped that she was compelled to change her position. She leaned back upon her elbow, determined to rise again and maintain her watch the moment she was rested. But sleep was close upon her. There was a lull in the louder noises of the jungle. Her eyes closed, and her head sank lower. In a little time it was lying upon Winthrope's shoulder, and she was fast asleep.

As Blake had asserted, the mosquitoes had either been blown away by the cyclone, or did not fly to such a height. None came to trouble the exhausted sleepers.

CHAPTER VI

MAN AND GENTLEMAN

Night had almost passed, and all three, soothed by the refreshing coolness which preceded the dawn, were sleeping their soundest, when a sudden fierce roar followed instantly by a piercing squeal caused even Blake to start up in panic. Miss Leslie, too terrified to scream, clung to Winthrope, who crouched on his haunches, little less overcome.

Blake was the first to recover and puzzle out the meaning of the crashing in the jungle and the ferocious growls directly beneath them.

"Lie still," he whispered. "We're all right. It's only a beast that's killed something down below us."

All sat listening, and as the noise of the animals in the thicket died away, they could hear the beast beneath them tear at the body of its victim.

"The air feels like dawn," whispered Winthrope. "We'll soon be able to see the brute."

"And he us," rejoined Blake.

In this both were mistaken. During the brief false dawn they were puzzled by the odd appearance of the ground. The sudden flood of full daylight found them staring down into a dense white fog.

"So they have that here!" muttered Blake—"fever-fog!"

"Beastly shame!" echoed Winthrope. "I'm sure the creature has gone off."

This assertion was met by an outburst of snarls and yells that made all start back and crouch down again in their sheltering hollow. As before, Blake was the first to recover.

"Bet you're right," he said. "The big one has gone off, and a pack of these African coyotes are having a scrap over the bones."

"You mean jackals. It sounds like the nasty beasts."

"If it wasn't for that fog, I'd go down and get our share of the game."

"Would it not be very dangerous, Mr. Blake?" asked Miss Leslie. "What a fearful noise!"

"I've chased coyotes off a calf with a rope; but that's not the proposition. You don't find me fooling around in that sewer gas of a fog. We'll roost right where we are till the sun does for it. We've got enough malaria in us already."

"Will it be long, Blake?" asked Winthrope.

"Huh? Getting hungry this quick? Wait till you've tramped around a week, with nothing to eat but your shoes."

"Surely, Mr. Blake, it will not be so bad!" protested Miss Leslie.

"Sorry, Miss Jenny; but cocoanut palms don't blow over every day, and when those nuts are gone, what are we going to do for the next meal?"

"Could we not make bows?" suggested Winthrope. "There seems to be no end of game about."

"Bows—and arrows without points! Neither of us could hit a barn door, anyway."

"We could practise."

"Sure—six weeks' training on air pudding. I can do better with a handful of stones."

"Then we should go at once to the cliffs," said Miss Leslie.

"Now you're talking—and it's Pike Peak or bust, for ours. Here's one night to the good; but we won't last many more if we don't get fire. It's flints we're after now."

"Could we not make fire by rubbing sticks?" said Winthrope, recalling his suggestion of the previous morning. "I've heard that natives have no trouble—"

"So've I, and what's more, I've seen 'em do it. Never could make a go of it myself, though."

"But if you remember how it is done, we have at least some chance—"

"Give you ten to one odds! No; we'll scratch around for a flint good and plenty before we waste time that way."

"The mist is going," observed Miss Leslie.

"That's no lie. Now for our coyotes. Where's my club?"

"They've all left," said Winthrope, peering down. "I can see the ground clearly, and there is not a sign of the beasts."

"There are the bones—what's left of them," added Blake. "It's a small deer, I suppose. Well, here goes."

He threw down his club, and dropped the loose end of the creeper after it. As the line straightened, he twisted the upper part around his leg, and was about to slide to the ground, when he remembered Miss Leslie.

"Think you can make it alone?" he asked.

The girl held up her hands, sore and swollen from the lacerations of the thorns. Blake looked at them, frowned, and turned to Winthrope.

"Um! you got it, too, and in the face," he grunted. "How's your ankle?"

Winthrope wriggled his foot about, and felt the injured ankle.

"I fancy it is much better," he answered. "There seems to be no swelling, and there is no pain now."

"That's lucky; though it will tune up later. Take a slide, now. We've got to hustle our breakfast, and find a way to get over the river."

"How wide is it?" inquired Winthrope, gazing at his swollen hands.

"About three hundred yards at high tide. May be narrower at ebb."

"Could you not build a raft?" suggested Miss Leslie.

Blake smiled at her simplicity. "Why not a boat? We've got a penknife."

"Well, then, I can swim."

"Bully for you! Guess, though, we'll try something else. The river is chuck full of alligators. What you waiting for, Pat? We haven't got all day to fool around here."

Winthrope twisted the creeper about his leg and slid to the ground, doing all he could to favor his hands. He found that he could walk without pain, and at once stepped over beside Blake's club, glancing nervously around at the jungle.

Blake jerked up the end of the creeper, and passed the loop about Miss Leslie. Before she had time to become frightened, he swung her over and lowered her to the ground lightly as a feather. He followed, hand under hand, and stood for a moment beside her, staring at the dew-dripping foliage of the jungle. Then the remains of the night's quarry caught his eye, and he walked over to examine them.

"Say, Pat," he called, "these don't look like deer bones. I'd say— yes; there's the feet—it's a pig."

"Any tusks?" demanded Winthrope.

Miss Leslie looked away. A heap of bones, however cleanly gnawed, is not a pleasant sight. The skull of the animal seemed to be missing; but Blake stumbled upon it in a tuft of grass, and kicked it out upon the open ground. Every shred of hide and gristle had been gnawed from it by the jackals; yet if there had been any doubt as to the creature's identity, there was evidence to spare in the savage tusks which projected from the jaws.

"Je-rusalem!" observed Blake; "this old boar must have been something of a scrapper his own self."

"In India they have been known to kill a tiger. Can you knock out the tusks?"

"What for?"

"Well, you said we had nothing for arrow points—"

"Good boy! We'll cinch them, and ask questions later."

A few blows with the club loosened the tusks. Blake handed them over to Winthrope, together with the whiskey flask, and led the way to the half-broken path through the thicket. A free use of his club made the path a little more worthy of the name, and as there was less need of haste than on the previous evening, Winthrope and Miss Leslie came through with only a few fresh scratches. Once on open ground again, they soon gained the fallen palms.

At a word from Blake, Miss Leslie hastened to fetch nuts for Winthrope to husk and open. Blake, who had plucked three leaves from a fan palm near the edge of the jungle, began to split long shreds from one of the huge leaves of a cocoanut palm. This gave him a quantity of coarse, stiff fibre, part of which he twisted in a cord and used to tie one of the leaves of the fan palm over his head.

"How's that for a bonnet?" he demanded.

The improvised head-gear bore so grotesque a resemblance to a recent type of picture hat that Winthrope could not repress a derisive laugh. Miss Leslie, however, examined the hat and gave her opinion without a sign of amusement. "I think it is splendid, Mr. Blake. If we must go out in the sun again, it is just the thing to protect one."

"Yes. Here's two more I've fixed for you. Ready yet, Winthrope?"

The Englishman nodded, and the three sat down to their third feast of cocoanuts. They were hungry enough at the start, and Blake added no little keenness even to his own appetite by a grim joke on the slender prospects of the next meal, to the effect that, if in the meantime not eaten themselves, they might possibly find their next meal within a week.

"But if we must move, could we not take some of the nuts with us?" suggested Winthrope.

Blake pondered over this as he ate, and when, fully satisfied, he helped himself up with his club, he motioned the others to remain seated.

"There are your hats and the strings," he said, "but you won't need them now. I'm going to take a prospect along the river; and while I'm gone, you can make a try at stringing nuts on some of this leaf fibre."

"But, Mr. Blake, do you think it's quite safe?" asked Miss Leslie, and she glanced from him to the jungle.

"Safe?" he repeated. "Well, nothing ate you yesterday, if that's anything to go by. It's all I know about it."

He did not wait for further protests. Swinging his club on his shoulder, he started for the break in the jungle which marked the hippopotamus path. The others looked at each other, and Miss Leslie sighed.

"If only he were a gentleman!" she complained.

Winthrope turned abruptly to the cocoanuts.

CHAPTER VII

AROUND THE HEADLAND

It was mid morning before Blake reappeared. He came from the mangrove swamp where it ran down into the sea. His trousers were smeared to the thigh with slimy mud; but as he approached, the drooping brim of his palm-leaf hat failed to hide his exultant expression.

"Come on!" he called. "I've struck it. We'll be over in half an hour."

"How's that?" asked Winthrope.

"Bar," answered Blake, hurrying forward. "Sling on your hats, and get into my coat again, Miss Jenny. The sun's hot as yesterday. How about the nuts?"

"Here they are. Three strings; all that I fancied we could carry," explained Winthrope.

"All right. The big one is mine, I suppose. I'll take two. We'll leave the other. Lean on me, if your ankle is still weak."

"Thanks; I can make it alone. But must we go through mud like that?"

"Not on this side, at least. Come on! We don't want to miss the ebb."

Blake's impatience discouraged further inquiries. He had turned as he spoke, and the others followed him, walking close together. The pace was sharp for Winthrope, and his ankle soon began to twinge. He was compelled to accept Miss Leslie's invitation to take her arm. With her help, he managed to keep within a few yards of Blake.

Instead of plunging into the mangrove wood, which here was undergrown with a thicket of giant ferns, Blake skirted around in the open until they came to the seashore. The tide was at its lowest, and he waved his club towards a long sand spit which curved out around the seaward edge of the mangroves. Whether this was part of the river's bar, or had been heaped up by the cyclone would have been beyond Winthrope's knowledge, had the question occurred to him. It was enough for him that the sand was smooth and hard as a race track.

Presently the party came to the end of the spit, where the river water rippled over the sand with the last feeble out-suck of the ebb. On their right they had a sweeping view of the river, around the flank of the mangrove screen. Blake halted at the edge of the water, and half turned.

44

"Close up," he said. "It's shallow enough; but do you see those logs over on the mud-bank? Those are alligators."

"Mercy!—and you expect me to wade among such creatures?" cried Miss Leslie.

"I went almost across an hour ago, and they didn't bother me any. Come on! There's wind in that cloud out seaward. Inside half an hour the surf'll be rolling up on this bar like all Niagara."

"If we must, we must, Miss Genevieve," urged Winthrope. "Step behind me, and gather up your skirts. It's best to keep one's clothes dry in the tropics."

The girl blushed, and retained his arm.

"I prefer to help you," she replied.

"Come on!" called Blake, and he splashed out into the water.

The others followed within arm's-length, nervously conscious of the rows of motionless reptiles on the mud-flat, not a hundred yards distant.

In the centre of the bar, where the water was a trifle over knee-deep, some large creature came darting down-stream beneath the surface, and passed with a violent swirl between Blake and his companions. At Miss Leslie's scream, Blake whirled about and jabbed with his club at the supposed alligator.

"Where's the brute? Has he got you?" he shouted.

"No, no; he went by!" gasped Winthrope. "There he is!"

A long bony snout, fringed on either side by a row of lateral teeth, was flung up into view.

"Sawfish!" said Blake, and he waded on across the bar, without further comment.

Miss Leslie had been on the point of fainting. The tone of Blake's voice revived her instantly.

There were no more scares. A few minutes later they waded out upon a stretch of clean sand on the south side of the river. Before them the beach lay in a flattened curve, which at the far end hooked sharply to the left, and appeared to terminate at the foot of the towering limestone cliffs of the headland. A mile or more inland the river jungle edged in close to the cliffs; but from there to the beach the forest was separated from the wall of rock by a little sandy plain, covered with creeping plants and small palms. The greatest width of the open space was hardly more than a quarter of a mile.

Blake paused for a moment at high-tide mark, and Winthrope instantly squatted down to nurse his ankle.

45

"I say, Blake," he said, "can't you find me some kind of a crutch? It is only a few yards around to those trees."

"Good Lord! you haven't been fool enough to overstrain that ankle– Yes, you have. Dammit! why couldn't you tell me before?"

"It did not feel so painful in the water."

"I helped the best I could," interposed Miss Leslie. "I think if you could get Mr. Winthrope a crutch–"

"Crutch!" growled Blake. "How long do you think it would take me to wade through the mud? And look at that cloud! We're in for a squall. Here!"

He handed the girl the smaller string of cocoanuts, flung the other up the beach, and stooped for Winthrope to mount his back. He then started off along the beach at a sharp trot. Miss Leslie followed as best she could, the heavy cocoanuts swinging about with every step and bruising her tender body.

The wind was coming faster than Blake had calculated. Before they had run two hundred paces, they heard the roar of rain-lashed water, and the squall struck them with a force that almost overthrew the girl. With the wind came torrents of rain that drove through their thickest garments and drenched them to the skin within the first half-minute.

Blake slackened his pace to a walk, and plodded sullenly along beneath the driving down-pour. He kept to the lower edge of the beach, where the sand was firmest, for the force of the falling deluge beat down the waves and held in check the breakers which the wind sought to roll up the beach.

The rain storm was at its height when they reached the foot of the cliffs. The gray rock towered above them, thirty or forty feet high. Blake deposited Winthrope upon a wet ledge, and straightened up to scan the headland. Here and there ledges ran more than half-way up the rocky wall; in other places the crest was notched by deep clefts; but nowhere within sight did either offer a continuous path to the summit. Blake grunted with disgust.

"It'd take a fire ladder to get up this side," he said. "We'll have to try the other, if we can get around the point. I'm going on ahead. You can follow, after Pat has rested his ankle. Keep a sharp eye out for anything in the flint line—quartz or agate. That means fire. Another thing, when this rain blows over, don't let your clothes dry on you. I've got my hands full enough, without having to nurse you through malarial fever. Don't forget the cocoanuts, and if I don't show up by noon, save me some."

He stooped to drink from a pool in the rock which was overflowing with the cool, pure rainwater, and started off at his sharpest pace. Winthrope and Miss Leslie, seated side by side in dripping misery, watched him swing away through the rain, without energy enough to call out a parting word.

Beneath the cliff the sand beach was succeeded by a talus of rocky debris which in places sloped up from the water ten or fifteen feet. The lower part of the slope consisted of boulders and water-worn stones, over which the surf, reinforced by the rising tide, was beginning to break with an angry roar.

Blake picked his way quickly over the smaller stones near the top of the slope, now and then bending to snatch up a fragment that seemed to differ from the others. Finding nothing but limestone, he soon turned his attention solely to the passage around the headland. Here he had expected to find the surf much heavier. But the shore was protected by a double line of reefs, so close in that the channel between did not show a whitecap. This was fortunate, since in places the talus here sank down almost to the level of low tide. Even a moderate surf would have rendered farther progress impracticable.

Another hundred paces brought Blake to the second corner of the cliff, which jutted out in a little point. He clambered around it, and stopped to survey the coast beyond. Within the last few minutes the squall had blown over, and the rain began to moderate its down-pour. The sun, bursting through the clouds, told that the storm was almost past, and its flood of direct light cleared the view.

Along the south side of the cliff the sea extended in twice as far as on the north. From the end of the talus the coast trended off four or five miles to the south-southwest in a shallow bight, whose southern extremity was bounded by a second limestone headland. This ridge ran inland parallel to the first, and from a point some little distance back from the shore was covered with a growth of leafless trees.

Between the two ridges lay a plain, open along the shore, but a short distance inland covered with a jungle of tall yellow grass, above which, here and there, rose the tops of scrubby, leafless trees and the graceful crests of slender-shafted palms. Blake's attention was drawn to the latter by that feeling of artificiality which their exotic appearance so often wakens in the mind of the Northern-bred man even after long

47

residence in the tropics. But in a moment he turned away, with a growl. "More of those darned feather-dusters!" He was not looking for palms.

The last ragged bit of cloud, with its showery accompaniment, drifted past before the breeze which followed the squall, and the end of the storm was proclaimed by a deafening chorus of squawks and screams along the higher ledges of the cliff. Staring upward, Blake for the first time observed that the face of the cliff swarmed with seafowl.

"That's luck!" he muttered. "Guess I haven't forgot how to rob nests. Bet our fine lady'll shy at sucking them raw! All the same, she'll have to, if I don't run across other rock than this, poor girl!"

He advanced again along the talus, and did not stop until he reached the sand beach. There he halted to make a careful examination, not only of the loose debris, but of the solid rock above. Finding no sign of flint or quartz, he growled out a curse, and backed off along the beach, to get a view of the cliff top. From a point a little beyond him, outward to the extremity of the headland, he could see that the upper ledges and the crest of the cliff, as well, were fairly crowded with seafowl and their nests. His smile of satisfaction broadened when he glanced inland and saw, less than half a mile distant, a wooded cleft which apparently ran up to the summit of the ridge. From a point near the top a gigantic baobab tree towered up against the skyline like a Brobdingnagian cabbage.

"Say, we may have a run for our money, after all," he murmured. "Shade, and no end of grub, and, by the green of those trees, a spring— limestone water at that. Next thing, I'll find a flint!"

He slapped his leg, and both sound and feeling reminded him that his clothes were drenched.

"Guess we'll wait about that flint," he said, and he made for a clump of thorn scrub a little way inland.

As the tall grass did not grow here within a mile of the shore, there was nothing to obstruct him. The creeping plants which during the rainy season had matted over the sandy soil were now leafless and withered by the heat of the dry season. Even the thorn scrub was half bare of leaves.

Blake walked around the clump to the shadiest side, and began to strip. In quick succession, one garment after another was flung across a branch where the sun would strike it. Last of all, the shoes were emptied of rainwater and set out to dry. Without a pause, he then gave himself a quick, light rub-down, just sufficient to invigorate the skin without starting the perspiration.

48

Physically the man was magnificent. His muscles were wiry and compact, rather than bulky, and as he moved, they played beneath his white skin with the smoothness and ease of a tiger's.

After the rub-down, he squatted on his heels, and spent some time trying to bend his palm-leaf hat back into shape. When he had placed this also out in the sun, he found himself beginning to yawn. The dry, sultry air had made him drowsy. A touch with his bare foot showed him that the sand beneath the thorn bush had already absorbed the rain and offered a dry surface. He glanced around, drew his club nearer, and stretched himself out for a nap.

CHAPTER VIII

THE CLUB AGE

It was past two o'clock when the sun, striking in where Blake lay outstretched, began to scorch one of his legs. He stirred uneasily, and sat upright. Like a sailor, he was wide awake the moment he opened his eyes. He stood up, and peered around through the half leafless branches.

Over the water thousands of gulls and terns, boobies and cormorants were skimming and diving, while above them a number of graceful frigate birds—those swart, scarlet-throated pirates of the air,— hung poised, ready to swoop down and rob the weaker birds of their fish. All about the headland and the surrounding water was life in fullest action. Even from where he stood Blake could hear the harsh clamor of the seafowl.

In marked contrast to this scene, the plain was apparently lifeless. When Blake rose, a small brown lizard darted away across the sand. Otherwise there was neither sight nor sound of a living creature. Blake pondered this as he gathered his clothes into the shade and began to dress.

"Looks like the siesta is the all-round style in this God-forsaken hole," he grumbled. "Haven't seen so much as a rabbit, nor even one land bird. May be a drought—no; must be the dry season— Whee, these things are hot! I'm thirsty as a shark. Now, where's that softy and her Ladyship? 'Fraid she's in for a tough time!"

He drew on his shoes with a jerk, growled at their stiffness, and club in hand, stepped clear of the brush to look for his companions. The first glance along the foot of the cliff showed him Winthrope lying under the shade of the overhanging ledges, a few yards beyond the sand beach. Of Miss Leslie there was no sign. Half alarmed by this, Blake started for the beach with his swinging stride. Winthrope was awake, and on Blake's approach, sat up to greet him.

"Hello!" he called. "Where have you been all this time?"

"'Sleep. Where's Miss Leslie?"

"She's around the point."

Blake grinned mockingly. "Indeed! But I fawncy she won't be for long."

He would have passed on, but Winthrope stepped before him.

50

"Don't go out there, Blake," he protested. "I—ah—think it would be better if I went."

"Why?" demanded Blake.

Winthrope hesitated; but an impatient movement by Blake forced an answer: "Well, you remember, this morning, telling us to dry our clothes."

"Yes; I remember," said Blake. "So you want to serve as lady's valet?"

Winthrope's plump face turned a sickly yellow.

"I—ah—valet?—What do you mean, sir? I protest—I do not understand you!" he stammered. But in the midst, catching sight of Blake's bewildered stare, he suddenly flushed crimson, and burst out in unrestrained anger: "You—you bounder—you beastly cad! Any man with an ounce of decency—"

Blake uttered a jeering laugh— "Wow! Hark, how the British lion r-r-ro-ars when his tail's twisted!"

"You beastly cad!" repeated the Englishman, now purple with rage.

Blake's unpleasant pleasantry gave place to a scowl. His jaw thrust out like a bulldog's, and he bent towards Winthrope with a menacing look. For a moment the Englishman faced him, sustained by his anger. But there was a steely light in Blake's eyes that he could not withstand. Winthrope's defiant stare wavered and fell. He shrank back, the color fast ebbing from his cheeks.

"Ugh!" growled Blake. "Guess you won't blat any more about cads! You damned hypocrite! Maybe I'm not on to how you've been hanging around Miss Leslie just because she's an heiress. Anything is fair enough for you swells. But let a fellow so much as open his mouth about your exalted set, and it's perfectly dreadful, you know!"

He paused for a reply. Winthrope only drew back a step farther, and eyed him with a furtive, sidelong glance. This brought Blake back to his mocking jeer. "You'll learn, Pat, me b'y. There's lots of things'll show up different to you before we get through this picnic. For one thing, I'm boss here—president, congress, and supreme court. Understand?"

"By what right, may I ask?" murmured Winthrope.

"Right!" answered Blake. "That hasn't anything to do with the question—it's might. Back in civilized parts, your little crowd has the drop on my big crowd, and runs things to suit themselves. But here we've sort of reverted to primitive society. This happens to be the Club Age, and I'm the Man with the Big Stick. See?"

"I myself sympathize with the lower classes, Mr. Blake. Above all, I think it barbarous the way they punish one who is forced by circumstances to appropriate part of the ill-gotten gains of the rich upstarts. But do you believe, Mr. Blake, that brute strength—"

"You bet! Now shut up. Where're the cocoanuts?"

Winthrope picked up two nuts and handed them over.

"There were only five," he explained.

"All right. I'm no captain of industry."

"Ah, true; you said we had reverted to barbarism," rejoined Winthrope, venturing an attempt at sarcasm.

"Lucky for you!" retorted Blake. "But where's Miss Leslie all this time? Her clothes must have dried hours ago."

"They did. We had luncheon together just this side of the point."

"Oh, you did! Then why shouldn't I go for her?"

"I—I—there was a shaded pool around the point, and she thought a dip in the salt water would refresh her. She went not more than half an hour ago."

"So that's it. Well, while I eat, you go and call her—and say, you keep this side the point. I'm looking out for Miss Leslie now."

Winthrope hurried away, clenching his fists and almost weeping with impotent rage. Truly, matters were now very different from what they had been aboard ship. Fortunately he had not gone a dozen steps before Miss Leslie appeared around the corner of the cliff. He was scrambling along over the loose stones of the slope without the slightest consideration for his ankle. The girl, more thoughtful, waved to him to wait for her where he was.

As she approached, Blake's frown gave place to a look that made his face positively pleasant. He had already drained the cocoanuts; now he proceeded to smash the shells into small bits, that he might eat the meat, and at the same time keep his gaze on the girl. The cliff foot being well shaded by the towering wall of rock, she had taken off his coat, and was carrying it on her arm; so that there was nothing to mar the effect of her dainty openwork waist, with its elbow sleeves and graceful collar and the filmy veil of lace over the shoulders and bosom. Her skirt had been washed clean by the rain, and she had managed to stretch it into shape before drying.

Refreshed by a nap in the forenoon and by her salt-water dip, she showed more vivacity than at any time that Winthrope could remember during their acquaintance. Her suffering during and since the storm had left its mark in the dark circles beneath her hazel eyes, but this in no wise lessened their brightness; while the elasticity of her step showed that she had quite recovered her well-bred ease and grace of movement.

She bowed and smiled to the two men impartially. "Good-afternoon, gentlemen."

"Same to you, Miss Leslie!" responded Blake, staring at her with frank admiration. "You look fresh as a daisy."

Genial and sincere as was his tone, the familiarity jarred on her sensitive ear. She colored as she turned from him.

"Is there anything new, Mr. Winthrope?" she asked.

"I'm afraid not, Miss Genevieve. Like ourselves, Blake took a nap."

"Yes; but Blake first took a squint at the scenery. Just see if you've got everything, and fix your hats. We'll be in the sun for half a mile or so. Better get on the coat, Miss Leslie. It's hotter than yesterday."

"Permit me," said Winthrope.

Blake watched while the Englishman held the coat for the girl and rather fussily raised the collar about her neck and turned back the sleeves, which extended beyond the tips of her fingers. The American's face was stolid; but his glance took in every little look and act of his companions. He was not altogether unversed in the ways of good society, and it seemed to him that the Englishman was somewhat over-assiduous in his attentions.

"All ready, Blake," remarked Winthrope, finally, with a last lingering touch.

"'Bout time!" grunted Blake. "You're fussy as a tailor. Got the flask and cigarette case and the knife?"

"All safe, sir—er—all safe, Blake."

"Then you two follow me slow enough not to worry that ankle. I don't want any more of the pack-mule in mine."

"Where are we going, Mr. Blake?" exclaimed Miss Leslie. "You will not leave us again!"

"It's only a half-mile, Miss Jenny. There's a break in the ridge. I'm going on ahead to find if it's hard to climb."

"But why should we climb?"

"Food, for one thing. You see, this end of the cliff is covered with sea-birds. Another thing, I expect to strike a spring."

"Oh, I hope you do! The water in the rain pools is already warm."

"They'll be dry in a day or two. Say, Winthrope, you might fetch some of those stones—size of a ball. I used to be a fancy pitcher when I was a kid, and we might scare up a rabbit or something."

"I play cricket myself. But these stones—"

"Better'n a gun, when you haven't got the gun. Come on. We'll go in a bunch, after all, in case I need stones."

With due consideration for Winthrope's ankle,—not for Winthrope,—Blake set so slow a pace that the half-mile's walk consumed over half an hour. But his smouldering irritation was soon quenched when they drew near the green thicket at the foot of the cleft. In the almost deathlike stillness of mid-afternoon, the sound of trickling water came to their ears, clear and musical.

"A spring!" shouted Blake. "I guessed right. Look at those green plants and grass; there's the channel where it runs out in the sand and dries up."

The others followed him eagerly as he pushed in among the trees. They saw no running water, for the tiny rill that trickled down the ledges was matted over with vines. But at the foot of the slope lay a pool, some ten yards across, and overshadowed by the surrounding trees. There was no underbrush, and the ground was trampled bare as a floor.

"By Jove," said Winthrope; "see the tracks! There must have been a drove of sheep about."

"Deer, you mean," replied Blake, bending to examine the deeper prints at the edge of the pool. "These ain't sheep tracks. A lot of them are larger."

"Could you not uncover the brook?" asked Miss Leslie. "If animals have been drinking here, one would prefer cleaner water."

"Sure," assented Blake. "If you're game for a climb, and can wait a few minutes, we'll get it out of the spring itself. We've got to go up anyway, to get at our poultry yard."

"Here's a place that looks like a path," called Winthrope, who had circled about the edge of the pool to the farther side.

Blake ran around beside him, and stared at the tunnel-like passage which wound up the limestone ledges beneath the over-arching thickets.

"Odd place, is it not?" observed Winthrope. "Looks like a fox run, only larger, you know."

"Too low for deer, though—and their hoofs would have cut up the moss and ferns more. Let's get a close look."

As he spoke, Blake stooped and climbed a few yards up the trail to an overhanging ledge, four or five feet high. Where the trail ran up over this break in the slope the stone was bare of all vegetation. Blake laid his club on the top of the ledge, and was about to vault after it, when, directly beneath his nose, he saw the print of a great catlike paw, outlined in dried mud. At the same instant a deep growl came rumbling down the "fox run." Without waiting for a second warning, Blake drew his club to him, and crept back down the trail. His stealthy movements and furtive backward glances filled his companions with vague terror. He himself was hardly less alarmed.

"Get out of the trees—into the open!" he exclaimed in a hoarse whisper, and as they crept away, white with dread of the unknown danger, he followed at their heels, looking backward, his club raised in readiness to strike.

Once clear of the trees, Winthrope caught Miss Leslie by the hand, and broke into a run. In their terror, they paid no heed to Blake's command to stop. They had darted off so unexpectedly that he did not overtake them short of a hundred yards.

"Hold on!" he said, gripping Winthrope roughly by the shoulder. "It's safe enough here, and you'll knock out that blamed ankle."

"What is it? What did you see?" gasped Miss Leslie.

"Footprint," mumbled Blake, ashamed of his fright.

"A lion's?" cried Winthrope.

"Not so large—'bout the size of a puma's. Must be a leopard's den up there. I heard a growl, and thought it about time to clear out."

"By Jove, we'd better withdraw around the point!"

"Withdraw your aunty! There's no leopard going to tackle us out here in open ground this time of day. The sneaking tomcat! If only I had a match, I'd show him how we smoke rat holes."

"Mr. Winthrope spoke of rubbing sticks to make fire," suggested Miss Leslie.

"Make sweat, you mean. But we may as well try it now, if we're going to at all. The sun's hot enough to fry eggs. We'll go back to a shady place, and pick up sticks on the way."

Though there was shade under the cliff within some six hundred feet, they had to go some distance to the nearest dry wood—a dead thorp-bush. Here they gathered a quantity of branches, even Miss Leslie volunteering to carry a load.

All was thrown down in a heap near the cliff, and Blake squatted beside it, penknife in hand. Having selected the dryest of the larger sticks, he bored a hole in one side and dropped in a pinch of powdered bark. Laying the stick in the full glare of the sun, he thrust a twig into the hole, and began to twirl it between his palms. This movement he kept up for several minutes; but whether he was unable to twirl the twig fast enough, or whether the right kind of wood or tinder was lacking, all his efforts failed to produce a spark.

Unwilling to accept the failure, Winthrope insisted upon trying in turn, and pride held him to the task until he was drenched with sweat. The result was the same.

"Told you so," jeered Blake from where he. lay in the shade. "We'd stand more chance cracking stones together."

"But what shall we do now?" asked Miss Leslie. "I am becoming very tired of cocoanuts, and there seems to be nothing else around here. Indeed, I think this is all such a waste of time. If we had walked straight along the shore this morning we might have reached a town."

"We might, Miss Jenny, and then, again, we mightn't. I happened to overhaul the captain's chart—Quilimane, Mozambique—that's all for hundreds of miles. Towns on this coast are about as thick as hens'-teeth."

"How about native villages?" demanded Winthrope.

"Oh, yes; maybe I'm fool enough to go into a wild nigger town without a gun. Maybe I didn't talk with fellows down on the Rand."

"But what shall we do?" repeated Miss Leslie, with a little frightened catch in her voice. She was at last beginning to realize what this rude break in her sheltered, pampered life might mean. "What shall we do? It's—it's absurd to think of having to stay in this horrid country for weeks or perhaps months—unless some ship comes for us!"

"Look here, Miss Leslie," answered Blake, sharply yet not unkindly; "suppose you just sit back and use your thinker a bit. If you're your daddy's daughter, you've got brains somewhere down under the boarding-school stuff."

"What do you mean, sir?"

"Now, don't get huffy, please! It's a question of think, not of putting on airs. Here we are, worse off than the people of the Stone Age. They had fire and flint axes; we've got nothing but our think tanks, and as to lions and leopards and that sort of thing, it strikes me we've got about as many on hand as they had."

"Then you and Mr. Winthrope should immediately arm yourselves."

"How?—But we'll leave that till later. What else?"

56

The girl gazed at the surrounding objects, her forehead wrinkled in the effort at concentration. "We must have water. Think how we suffered yesterday! Then there is shelter from wild beasts, and food, and—"

"All right here under our hands, if we had fire. Understand?"

"I understand about the water. You would frighten the leopard away with the fire; and if it would do that, it would also keep away the other animals at night. But as for food, unless we return for cocoanuts—"

"Don't give it up! Keep your thinker going on the side, while Pat tells us our next move. Now that he's got the fire sticks out of his head—"

"I say, Blake, I wish you would drop that name. It is no harder to say Winthrope."

"You're off, there," rejoined Blake. "But look here, I'll make it Win, if you figure out what we ought to do next."

"Really, Blake, that would not be half bad. They—er—they called me Win at Harrow."

"That so? My English chum went to Harrow—Jimmy Scarbridge."

"Lord James!—your chum?"

"He started in like you, sort of top-lofty. But he chummed all right—after I took out a lot of his British starch with a good walloping."

"Oh, really now, Blake, you can't expect any one with brains to believe that, you know!"

"No; I don't know, you know,—and I don't know if you've got any brains, you know. Here's your chance to show us. What's our next move?"

"Really, now, I have had no experience in this sort of thing—don't interrupt, please! It seems to me that our first concern is shelter for the night. If we should return to your tree nest, we should also be near the cocoa palms."

"That's one side. Here's the other. Bar to wade across—sharks and alligators; then swampy ground—malaria, mosquitoes, thorn jungle. Guess the hands of both of you are still sore enough, by their look."

"If only I had a pot of cold cream!" sighed Miss Leslie.

"If only I had a hunk of jerked beef!" echoed Blake.

"I say, why couldn't we chance it for the night around on the seaward face of the cliff?" asked Winthrope. "I noticed a place where the ledges overhang—almost a cave. Do you think it probable that any wild beast would venture so close to the sea?"

"Can't say. Didn't see any tracks; so we'll chance it for to-night. Next!"

"By morning I believe my ankle will be in such shape that I could go back for the string of cocoanuts which we dropped on the beach."

"I'll go myself, to-day, else we'll have no supper. Now we're getting down to bedrock. If those nuts haven't been washed away by the tide, we're fixed for to-night; and for two meals, such as they are. But what next? Even the rain pools will be dried up by another day or so."

"Are not sea-birds good to eat?" inquired Miss Leslie.

"Some."

"Then, if only we could climb the cliff—might there not be another place?"

"No; I've looked at both sides. What's more, that spotted tomcat has got a monopoly on our water supply. The river may be fresh at low tide; but we've got nothing to boil water in, and such bayou stuff is just concentrated malaria."

"Then we must find water elsewhere," responded Miss Leslie. "Might we not succeed if we went on to the other ridge?"

"That's the ticket! You've got a headpiece, Miss Jenny! It's too late to start now. But first thing to-morrow I'll take a run down that way, while you two lay around camp and see if you can twist some sort of fish-line out of cocoanut fibre. By braiding your hair, Miss Jenny, you can spare us your hair-pins for hooks."

"But, Mr. Blake, I'm afraid—I'd rather you'd take us with you. With that dreadful creature so near—"

"Well, I don't know. Let's see your feet?"

Miss Leslie glanced at him, and thrust a slender foot from beneath her skirt.

"Um-m—stocking torn; but those slippers are tougher than I thought. Most of the way will be good walking, along the beach. We'll leave the fishing to Pat—er—beg pardon—Win! With his ankle—"

"By Jove, Blake, I'll chance the ankle. Don't leave me behind. I give you my word, you'll not have to lug me."

"Oh, of course, Mr. Winthrope must go with us!"

"'Fraid to go alone, eh?" demanded Blake, frowning.

His tone startled and offended her; yet all he saw was a politely quizzical lifting of her brows.

"Why should I be afraid, Mr. Blake?" she asked.

Blake stared at her moodily. But when she met his gaze with a confiding smile, he flushed and looked away.

"All right," he muttered; "well move camp together. But don't expect me to pack his ludship, if we draw a blank and have to trek back without food or water."

CHAPTER IX

THE LEOPARDS' DEN

While Blake made a successful trip for the abandoned cocoanuts, his companions levelled the stones beneath the ledges chosen by Winthrope, and gathered enough dried sea-weed along the talus to soften the hard beds.

Soothed by the monotonous wash of the sea among the rocks, even Miss Leslie slept well. Blake, who had insisted that she should retain his coat, was wakened by the chilliness preceding the dawn. Five minutes later they started on their journey.

The starlight glimmered on the waves and shed a faint radiance over the rocks. This and their knowledge of the way enabled them to pick a path along the foot of the cliff without difficulty. Once on the beach, they swung along at a smart gait, invigorated by the cool air.

Dawn found them half way to their goal. Blake called a halt when the first red streaks shot up the eastern sky. All stood waiting until the quickly following sun sprang forth from the sea. Blake's first act was to glance from one headland to the other, estimating their relative distances. His grunt of satisfaction was lost in Winthrope's exclamation, "By Jove, look at the cattle!"

Blake and Miss Leslie turned to stare at the droves of animals moving about between them and the border of the tall grass. Miss Leslie was the first to speak. "They can't be cattle, Mr. Winthrope. There are some with stripes. I do believe they're zebras!"

"Get down!" commanded Blake. "They're all wild game. Those big ox-like fellows to the left of the zebras are eland. Whee! wouldn't we be in it if we owned that water hole? I'll bet I'd have one of those fat beeves inside three days."

"How I should enjoy a juicy steak!" murmured Miss Leslie.

"Raw or jerked?" questioned Blake.

"What is 'jerked'?"

"Dried."

"Oh, no; I mean broiled—just red inside."

"I prefer mine quite rare," added Winthrope.

"That's the way you'll get it, damned rare—Beg your pardon, Miss Jenny! Without fire, we'll have the choice of raw or jerked."

"Horrors!"

"Jerked meat is all right. You cut your game in strips—"

"With a penknife!" laughed Miss Leslie.

Blake stared at her glumly. "That's so. You've got it back on me—Butcher a beef with a penknife! We'll have to take it raw, and dog-fashion at that."

"Haven't I heard of bamboo knives?" said Winthrope.

"Bamboo?"

"I'm sure I can't say, but as I remember, it seems to me that the varnish-like glaze—"

"Silica? Say, that would cut meat. But where in—where in hades are the bamboos?"

"I'm sure I can't say. Only I remember that I have seen them in other tropical places, you know."

"Meantime I prefer cocoanuts, until we have a fire to broil our steaks," remarked Miss Leslie.

"Ditto, Miss Jenny, long's we have the nuts and no meat. I'm a vegetarian now—but maybe my mouth ain't watering for something else. Look at all those chops and roasts and stews running around out there!"

"They are making for the grass," observed Winthrope. "Hadn't we better start?"

"Nuts won't weigh so much without the shells. We'll eat right here."

There were only a few nuts left. They were drained and cracked and scooped out, one after another. The last chanced to break evenly across the middle.

"Hello," said Blake, "the lower part of this will do for a bowl, Miss Jenny. When you've eaten the cream, put it in your pocket. Say, Win, have you got the bottle and keys and—"

"All safe—everything."

"Are you sure, Mr. Winthrope?" asked Miss Leslie. "Men's pockets seem so open. Twice I've had to pick up Mr. Blake's locket."

"Locket?" echoed Blake.

"The ivory locket. Women may be curious, Mr. Blake, but I assure you, I did not look inside, though—"

"Let me—give it here—quick!" gasped Blake.

Startled by his tone and look, Miss Leslie caught an oval object from the side pocket of the coat, and thrust it into Blake's outstretched hand. For a moment he stared at it, unable to believe his eyes; then he leaped up, with a yell that sent the droves of zebras and antelope flying into the tall grass.

"Oh! oh!" screamed Miss Leslie. "Is it a snake? Are you bitten?"

61

"Bitten?—Yes, by John Barleycorn! Must have been fuzzy drunk to put it in my coat. Always carry it in my fob pocket. What a blasted infernal idiot I've been! Kick me, Win,—kick me hard!"

"I say, Blake, what is it? I don't quite take you. If you would only—"

"Fire!—*fire!* Can't you see? We've got all hell beat! Look here."

He snapped open the slide of the supposed locket, and before either of his companions could realize what he would be about, was focussing the lens of a surveyor's magnifying-glass upon the back of Winthrope's hand. The Englishman jerked the hand away—

"*Ow!* That burns!"

Blake shook the glass in their bewildered faces.

"Look there!" he shouted, "there's fire; there's water; there's birds' eggs and beefsteaks! Here's where we trek on the back trail. We'll smoke out that leopard in short order!"

"You don't mean to say, Blake—"

"No; I mean to do! Don't worry. You can hide with Miss Jenny on the point, while I engineer the deal. Fall in."

The day was still fresh when they found themselves back at the foot of the cliff. Here arose a heated debate between the men. Winthrope, stung by Blake's jeering words, insisted upon sharing the attack, though with no great enthusiasm. Much to Blake's surprise, Miss Leslie came to the support of the Englishman.

"But, Mr. Blake," she argued, "you say it will be perfectly safe for us here. If so, it will be safe for myself alone."

"I can play this game without him."

"No doubt. Yet if, as you say, you expect to keep off the leopard with a torch, would it not be well to have Mr. Winthrope at hand with other torches, should yours burn out?"

"Yes; if I thought he'd be at hand after the first scare."

Winthrope started off, almost on a run. At that moment he might have faced the leopard single-handed. Blake chuckled as he swung away after his victim. Within ten paces, however, he paused to call back over his shoulder: "Get around the point, Miss Jenny, and if you want something to do, try braiding the cocoanut fibre."

Miss Leslie made no response; but she stood for some time gazing after the two men. There was so much that was characteristic even in this rear view. For all his anger and his haste, the Englishman bore himself with an air of well-bred nicety. His trim, erect figure needed only a fresh suit to be irreproachable. On the other hand, a careless observer, at first glance, might have mistaken Blake, with his flannel shirt and shouldered club, for a hulking navvy. But there was nothing of the navvy in his swinging stride or in the resolute poise of his head as he came up with Winthrope.

Though the girl was not given to reflection, the contrast between the two could not but impress her. How well her countryman—coarse, uncultured, but full of brute strength and courage—fitted in with these primitive surroundings. Whereas Winthrope . . . . and herself . . . .

She fell into a kind of disquieted brown study. Her eyes had an odd look, both startled and meditative,—such a look as might be expected of one who for the first time is peering beneath the surface of things, and sees the naked Realities of Life, the real values, bared of masking conventions. It may have been that she was seeking to ponder the meaning of her own existence—that she had caught a glimpse of the vanity and wastefulness, the utter futility of her life. At the best, it could only have been a glimpse. But was not that enough?

"Of what use are such people as I?" she cried. "That man may be rough and coarse,—even a brute; but he at least does things—I'll show him that I can do things, too!"

She hastened out around the corner of the cliff to the spot where they had spent the night. Here she gathered together the cocoanut husks, and seating herself in the shade of the overhanging ledges, began to pick at the coarse fibre. It was cruel work for her soft fingers, not yet fully healed from the thorn wounds. At times the pain and an overpowering sense of injury brought tears to her eyes; still more often she dropped the work in despair of her awkwardness. Yet always she returned to the task with renewed energy.

After no little perseverance, she found how to twist the fibre and plait it into cord. At best it was slow work, and she did not see how she should ever make enough cord for a fish-line. Yet, as she caught the knack of the work and her fingers became more nimble, she began to enjoy the novel pleasure of producing something.

She had quite forgot to feel injured, and was learning to endure with patience the rasping of the fibre between her fingers, when Winthrope came clambering around the corner of the cliff.

"What is it?" she exclaimed, springing up and hurrying to meet him. He was white and quivering, and the look in his eyes filled her with dread.

Her voice shrilled to a scream, "He's dead!"

Winthrope shook his head.

"Then he's hurt!—he's hurt by that savage creature, and you've run off and left him—"

"No, no, Miss Genevieve, I must insist! The fellow is not even scratched."

"Then why—?"

"It was the horror of it all. It actually made me ill."

"You frightened me almost to death. Did the beast chase you?"

"That would have been better, in a way. Really, it was horrible! I'm still sick over it, Miss Genevieve."

"But tell me about it. Did you set fire to the bushes in the cleft, as Mr. Blake—"

"Yes; after we had fetched what we could carry of that long grass—two big trusses. It grows ten or twelve feet tall, and is now quite dry. Part of it Blake made into torches, and we fired the bush all across the foot of the cleft. Really, one would not have thought there was that much dry wood in so green a dell. On either side of the rill the grass and brush flared like tinder, and the flames swept up the cleft far quicker than we had expected. We could hear them crackling and roaring louder than ever after the smoke shut out our view."

"Surely, there is nothing so very horrible in that."

"No, oh, no; it was not that. But the beast—the leopard! At first we heard one roar; then it was that dreadful snarling and yelling—most awful squalling! . . . . The wretched thing came leaping and tumbling down the path, all singed and blinded. Blake fired the big truss of grass, and the brute rolled right into the flames. It was shocking—dreadfully shocking! The wretched creature writhed and leaped about till it plunged into the pool. . . . . When it sought to crawl out, all black and hideous, Blake went up and killed it with his club—crushed in its skull—Ugh!"

Miss Leslie gazed at the unnerved Englishman with calm scrutiny.

"But why should you feel so about it?" she asked. "Was it not the beast's life against ours?"

"But so horrible a death!"

"I'm sure Mr. Blake would have preferred to shoot the creature, had he a gun. Having nothing else than fire, I think it was all very brave of him. Now we are sure of water and food. Had we not best be going?"

"It was to fetch you that Blake sent me."

Winthrope spoke with perceptible stiffness. He was chagrined, not only by her commendation of Blake, but by the indifference with which she had met his agitation.

They started at once, Miss Leslie in the lead. As they rounded the point, she caught sight of the smoke still rising from the cleft. A little later she noticed the vultures which were streaming down out of the sky from all quarters other than seaward. Their focal point seemed to be the trees at the foot of the cleft. A nearer view showed that they were alighting in the thorn bushes on the south border of the wood.

Of Blake there was nothing to be seen until Miss Leslie, still in the lead, pushed in among the trees. There they found him crouched beside a small fire, near the edge of the pool. He did not look up. His eyes were riveted in a hungry stare upon several pieces of flesh, suspended over the flames on spits of green twigs.

"Hello!" he sang out, as he heard their footsteps. "Just in time, Miss Jenny. Your broiled steak'll be ready in short order."

"Oh, build up the fire! I'm simply ravenous!" she exclaimed, between impatience and delight.

Winthrope was hardly less keen; yet his hunger did not altogether blunt his curiosity.

"I say, Blake," he inquired, "where did you get the meat?"

"Stow it, Win, my boy. This ain't a packing house. The stuff may be tough, but it's not—er—the other thing. Here you are, Miss Jenny. Chew it off the stick."

Though Winthrope had his suspicions, he took the piece of half-burned flesh which Blake handed him in turn, and fell to eating without further question. As Blake had surmised, the roast proved far other than tender. Hunger, however, lent it a most appetizing flavor. The repast ended when there was nothing left to devour. Blake threw away his empty spit, and rose to stretch. He waited for Miss Leslie to swallow her last mouthful, and then began to chuckle.

"What's the joke?" asked Winthrope.

Blake looked at him solemnly.

"Well now, that was downright mean of me," he drawled; "after robbing them, to laugh at it!"

"Robbing who?"

"The buzzards."

"You've fed us on leopard meat! It's—it's disgusting!"

"I found it filling. How about you, Miss Jenny?"

65

Miss Leslie did not know whether to laugh or to give way to a feeling of nausea. She did neither.

"Can we not find the spring of which you spoke?" she asked. "I am thirsty."

"Well, I guess the fire is about burnt out," assented Blake. "Come on; we'll see."

The cleft now had a far different aspect from what it had presented on their first visit. The largest of the trees, though scorched about the base, still stood with unwithered foliage, little harmed by the fire. But many of their small companions had been killed and partly destroyed by the heat and flames from the burning brush. In places the fire was yet smouldering.

Blake picked a path along the edge of the rill, where the moist vegetation, though scorched, had refused to burn. After the first abrupt ledge, up which Blake had to drag his companions, the ascent was easy. But as they climbed around an outjutting corner of the steep right wall of the cleft, Blake muttered a curse of disappointment. He could now see that the cleft did not run to the top of the cliff, but through it, like a tiny box canyon. The sides rose sheer and smooth as walls. Midway, at the highest point of the cleft, the baobab towered high above the ridge crest, its gigantic trunk filling a third of the breadth of the little gorge. Unfortunately it stood close to the left wall.

"Here's luck for you!" growled Blake. "Why couldn't the blamed old tree have grown on the other side? We might have found a way to climb it. Guess we'll have to smoke out another leopard. We're no nearer those birds' nests than we were yesterday."

"By Jove, look here!" exclaimed Winthrope. "This is our chance for antelope! Here by the spring are bamboos—real bamboos,—and only half the thicket burned."

"What of them?" demanded Blake.

"Bows—arrows—and did you not agree that they would make knives?"

"Umph—we'll see. What is it, Miss Jenny?"

"Isn't that a hole in the big tree?"

"Looks like it. These baobabs are often hollow."

"Perhaps that is where the leopard had his den," added Winthrope.

"Shouldn't wonder. We'll go and see."

"But, Mr. Blake," protested the girl, "may there not be other leopards?"

66

"Might have been; but I'll bet they lit out with the other. Look how the tree is scorched. Must have been stacks of dry brush around the hole, 'nough to smoke out a fireman. We'll look and see if they left any soup bones lying around. First, though, here's your drink, Miss Jenny."

As he spoke, Blake kicked aside some smouldering branches, and led the way to the crevice whence the spring trickled from the rock into a shallow stone basin. When all had drunk their fill of the clear cool water, Blake took up his club and walked straight across to the baobab. Less than thirty steps brought him to the narrow opening in the trunk of the huge tree. At first he could make out nothing in the dimly lit interior; but the fetid, catty odor was enough to convince him that he had found the leopards' den.

He caught the vague outlines of a long body, crouched five or six yards away, on the far side of the hollow. He sprang back, his club brandished to strike. But the expected attack did not follow. Blake glanced about as though considering the advisability of a retreat. Winthrope and Miss Leslie were staring at him, white-faced. The sight of their terror seemed to spur him to dare-devil bravado; though his actions may rather have been due to the fact that he realized the futility of flight, and so rose to the requirements of the situation—the grim need to stand and face the danger.

"Get behind the bamboos!" he called, and as they hurriedly obeyed, he caught up a stone and flung it in at the crouching beast.

He heard the missile strike with a soft thud that told him he had not missed his mark, and he swung up his club in both hands. Given half a chance, he would smash the skull of the female leopard as he had crushed her blinded mate. . . . . One moment after another passed, and he stood poised for the shock, tense and scowling. . . . . Not so much as a snarl came from within. The truth flashed upon him.

"Smothered!" he yelled.

The others saw him dart in through the hole. A moment later two limp grayish bodies were flung out into the open. Immediately after, Blake reappeared, dragging the body of the mother leopard.

"It's all right; they're dead!" cried Winthrope, and he ran forward to look at the bodies.

Miss Leslie followed, hardly less curious.

"Are they all dead, Mr. Blake?" she inquired.

"Wiped out—whole family. The old cat stayed by her kittens, and all smothered together—lucky for us! Get busy with those bamboos,

Win. I'm going to have these skins, and the sooner we get the cub meat hung up and curing, the better for us."

"Leopard meat again!" rejoined Winthrope.

"Spring leopard, young and tender! What more could you ask? Get a move on you."

"Can I do anything, Mr. Blake?" asked Miss Leslie.

"Hunt a shady spot."

"But I really mean it."

"Well, if that's straight, you might go on along the gully, and see if there's any place to get to the top. You could pick up sticks on the way back, if any are left. We'll have to fumigate this tree hole before we adopt it for a residence."

"Will it be long before you finish with your—with the bodies?"

"Well, now, look here, Miss Jenny; it's going to be a mess, and I wouldn't mind hauling the carcasses clear down the gully, out of sight, if it was to be the only time. But it's not, and you've got to get used to it, sooner or later. So we'll start now."

"I suppose, if I must, Mr. Blake— Really, I wish to help."

"Good. That's something like! Think you can learn to cook?"

"See what I did this morning."

Blake took the cord of cocoanut fibre which she held out to him, and tested its strength.

"Well, I'll be—blessed!" he said. "This *is* something like. If you don't look out, you'll make quite a camp-mate, Miss Jenny. But now, trot along. This is hardly arctic weather, and our abattoir don't include a cold-storage plant. The sooner these lambs are dressed, the better."

CHAPTER X

PROBLEMS IN WOODCRAFT

It was no pleasant sight that met Miss Leslie's gaze upon her return. The neatest of butchering can hardly be termed aesthetic; and Blake and Winthrope lacked both skill and tools. Between the penknife and an improvised blade of bamboo, they had flayed the two cubs and haggled off the flesh. The ragged strips, spitted on bamboo rods, were already searing in the fierce sun-rays.

Miss Leslie would have slipped into the hollow of the baobab with her armful of fagots and brush; but Blake waved a bloody knife above the body of the mother leopard, and beckoned the girl to come nearer.

"Hold on a minute, please," he said. "What did you find out?"

Miss Leslie drew a few steps nearer, and forced herself to look at the revolting sight. She found it still more difficult to withstand the odor of the fresh blood. Winthrope was pale and nauseated. The sight of his distress caused the girl to forget her own loathing. She drew a deep breath, and succeeded in countering Blake's expectant look with a half-smile.

"How well you are getting along!" she exclaimed.

"Didn't think you could stand it. But you've got grit all right, if you *are* a lady," Blake said admiringly. "Say, you'll make it yet! Now, how about the gully?"

"There is no place to climb up. It runs along like this, and then slopes down. But there is a cliff at the end, as high as these walls."

"Twenty feet," muttered Blake. "Confound the luck! It isn't that jump-off; but how in—how are we going to get up on the cliff? There's an everlasting lot of omelettes in those birds' nests. If only that bloomin'—how's that, Win, me b'y?—that bloomin', blawsted baobab was on t' other side. The wood's almost soft as punk. We could drive in pegs, and climb up the trunk."

"There are other trees beyond it," remarked Miss Leslie.

"Then maybe we can shin up—"

"I fear the branches that overhang the cliff are too slender to bear any weight."

"And it's too infernally high to climb up to this overhanging baobab limb."

"I say," ventured Winthrope, "if we had a axe, now, we might cut up one of the trees, and make a ladder."

"Oh, yes; and if we had a ladder, we might climb up the cliff!"

"But, Mr. Blake, is there not some way to cut down one of the trees? The tree itself would be a ladder if it fell in such a way as to lean against the cliff."

"There's only the penknife," answered Blake. "So I guess we'll have to scratch eggs off our menu card. Spring leopard for ours! Now, if you really want to help, you might scrape the soup bones out of your boudoir, and fetch a lot more brush. It'll take a big fire to rid the hole of that cat smell."

"Will not the tree burn?"

"No; these hollow baobabs have green bark on the inside as well as out. Funny thing, that! We'd have to keep a fire going a long time to burn through."

"Yet it would burn in time?"

"Yes; but we're not going to—"

"Then why not burn through the trunk of one of those small trees, instead of chopping it down?"

"By–heck, Miss Jenny, you've got an American headpiece! Come on. Sooner we get the thing started, the better."

Neither Winthrope nor Miss Leslie was reluctant to leave the vicinity of the carcasses. They followed close after Blake, around the monstrous bole of the baobab. A little beyond it stood a group of slender trees, whose trunks averaged eight inches thick at the base. Blake stopped at the second one, which grew nearest to the seaward side of the cleft.

"Here's our ladder," he said. "Get some firewood. Pound the bushes, though, before you go poking into them. May be snakes here."

"Snakes?–oh!" cried Miss Leslie, and she stood shuddering at the danger she had already incurred.

The fire had burnt itself out on a bare ledge of rock between them and the baobab, and the clumps of dry brush left standing in this end of the cleft were very suggestive of snakes, now that Blake had called attention to the possibility of their presence.

He laughed at his hesitating companions. "Go on, go on! Don't squeal till you're bit. Most snakes hike out, if you give them half a chance. Take a stick, each of you, and pound the bushes."

Thus urged, both started to work. But neither ventured into the thicker clumps. When they returned, with large armfuls of sticks and twigs, they found that Blake had used his glass to light a handful of dry bark, out in the sun, and was nursing it into a small fire at the base of the tree, on the side next the cliff.

"Now, Miss Jenny," he directed, "you're to keep this going—not too big a fire—understand? Same time you can keep on fetching brush to fumigate your cat hole. It needs it, all right."

"Will not that be rather too much for Miss Leslie?" asked Winthrope.

"Well, if she'd rather come and rub brains on the skins,—Indian tan, you know,—or—"

"How can you mention such things before a lady?" protested Winthrope.

"Beg your pardon, Miss Leslie! you see, I'm not much used to ladies' company. Anyway, you've got to see and hear about these things. And now I'll have to get the strings for Win's bamboo bows. Come on, Win. We've got that old tabby to peel, and a lot more besides."

Miss Leslie's first impulse was to protest against being left alone, when at any moment some awful venomous serpent might come darting at her out of the brush or the crevices in the rocks. But her half-parted lips drew firmly together, and after a moment's hesitancy, she forced herself to the task which had been assigned her. The fire, once started, required little attention. She could give most of her time to gathering brush for the fumigation of the leopard den.

She had collected quite a heap of fuel at the entrance of the hollow, when she remembered that the place would first have to be cleared of its accumulation of bones. A glance at her companions showed that they were in the midst of tasks even more revolting. It was certainly disagreeable to do such things; yet, as Mr. Blake had said, others had to do them. It was now her time to learn. She could see him smile at her hesitation.

Stung by the thought of his half contemptuous pity, she caught up a forked stick, and forced herself to enter the tree-cave. The stench met her like a blow. It nauseated and all but overpowered her. She stood for several moments in the centre of the cavity, sick and faint. Had it been even the previous day, she would have run out into the open air.

Presently she grew a little more accustomed to the stench, and began to rake over the soft dry mould of the den floor with her forked stick. Bones!—who had ever dreamed of such a mess of bones?—big bones and little bones and skulls; old bones, dry and almost buried;

71

mouldy bones; bones still half-covered with bits of flesh and gristle–the remnants of the leopard family's last meal.

At last all were scraped out and flung in a heap, three or four yards away from the entrance. Miss Leslie looked at the result of her labor with a satisfied glance, followed by a sigh of relief. Between the heat and her unwonted exercise, she was greatly fatigued. She stepped around to a shadier spot to rest.

With a start, she remembered the fire.

When she reached it there were only a few dying embers left. She gathered dead leaves and shreds of fibrous inner bark, and knelt beside the dull coals to blow them into life. She could not bear the thought of having to confess her carelessness to Blake.

The hot ashes flew up in her face and powdered her hair with their gray dust; yet she persisted, blowing steadily until a shred of bark caught the sparks and flared up in a tiny flame. A little more, and she had a strong fire blazing against the tree trunk.

She rested a short time, relaxing both mentally and physically in the satisfying consciousness that Blake never should know how near she had come to failing in her trust.

Soon she became aware of a keen feeling of thirst and hunger. She rose, piled a fresh supply of sticks on the fire, and hastened back through the cleft towards the spring. Around the baobab she came upon Winthrope, working in the shade of the great tree. The three leopard skins had been stretched upon bamboo frames, and he was resignedly scraping at their inner surfaces with a smooth-edged stone. Miss Leslie did not look too closely at the operation.

"Where is–he?" she asked.

Winthrope motioned down the cleft.

"I hope he hasn't gone far. I'm half famished. Aren't you?"

"Really, Miss Genevieve, it is odd, you know. Not an hour since, the very thought of food–"

"And now you're as hungry as I am. Oh, I do wish he had not gone off just at the wrong time!"

"He went to take a dip in the sea. You know, he got so messed up over the nastiest part of the work, which I positively refused to do–"

"What's that beyond the bamboos?–There's something alive!"

"Pray, don't be alarmed. It is–er–it's all right, Miss Genevieve, I assure you."

"But what is it? Such queer noises, and I see something alive!"

"Only the vultures, if you must know. Nothing else, I assure you."

"Oh!"

"It is all out of sight from the spring. You are not to go around the bamboos until the—that is, not to-day."

"Did Mr. Blake say that?"

"Why, yes—to be sure. He also said to tell you that the cutlets were on the top shelf."

"You mean —?"

"His way of ordering you to cook our dinner. Really, Miss Genevieve, I should be pleased to take your place, but I have been told to keep to this. It is hard to take orders from a low fellow,—very hard for a gentleman, you know."

Miss Leslie gazed at her shapely hands. Three days since she could not have conceived of their being so rough and scratched and dirty. Yet her disgust at their condition was not entirely unqualified.

"At least I have something to show for them," she murmured.

"I beg pardon," said Winthrope.

"Just look at my hands—like a servant's! And yet I am not nearly so ashamed of them as I would have fancied. It is very amusing, but do you know, I actually feel proud that I have done something—something useful, I mean."

"Useful?—I call it shocking, Miss Genevieve. It is simply vile that people of our breeding should be compelled to do such menial work. They write no end of romances about castaways; but I fail to see the romance in scraping skins Indian fashion, as this fellow Blake calls it."

"I suppose, though, we should remember how much Mr. Blake is doing for us, and should try to make the best of the situation."

"It has no best. It is all a beastly muddle," complained Winthrope, and he resumed his nervous scraping at the big leopard skin.

The girl studied his face for a moment, and turned away. She had been trying so hard to forget.

He heard her leave, and called after, without looking up: "Please remember. He said to cook some meat."

She did not answer. Having satisfied her thirst at the spring, she took one of the bamboo rods, with its haggled blackening pieces of flesh, and returned to the fire. After some little experimenting, she contrived a way to support the rod beside the fire so that all the meat would roast without burning.

At first, keen as was her hunger, she turned with disgust from the flabby sun-seared flesh; but as it began to roast, the odor restored her appetite to full vigor. Her mouth fairly watered. It seemed as though

Winthrope and Blake would never come. She heard their voices, and took the bamboo spit from the fire for the meat to cool. Still they failed to appear, and unable to wait longer, she began to eat. The cub meat proved far more tender than that of the old leopard. She had helped herself to the second piece before the two men appeared.

"Hold on, Miss Jenny; fair play!" sang out Blake. "You've set to without tooting the dinner-horn. I don't blame you, though. That smells mighty good."

Both men caught at the hot meat with eagerness, and Winthrope promptly forgot all else in the animal pleasure of satisfying his hunger. Blake, though no less hungry, only waited to fill his mouth before investigating the condition of the prospective tree ladder. The result of the attempt to burn the trunk did not seem encouraging to the others, and Miss Leslie looked away, that her face might not betray her, should he have an inkling of her neglect. She was relieved by the cheerfulness of his tone.

"Slow work, this fire business—eh? Guess, though, it'll go faster this afternoon. The green wood is killed and is getting dried out. Anyway, we've got to keep at it till the tree goes over. This spring leopard won't last long at the present rate of consumption, and we'll need the eggs to keep us going till we get the hang of our bows."

"What is that smoke back there?" interrupted Miss Leslie. "Can it be that the fire down the cleft has sprung up again?"

"No; it's your fumigation. You had plenty of brush on hand, so I heaved it into the hole, and touched it off. While it's burning out, you can put in time gathering grass and leaves for a bed."

"Would you and Mr. Winthrope mind breaking off some bamboos for me?"

"What for?"

Miss Leslie colored and hesitated. "I—I should like to divide off a corner of the place with a wall or screen."

Winthrope tried to catch Blake's eye; but the American was gazing at Miss Leslie's embarrassed face with a puzzled look. Her meaning dawned upon him, and he hastened to reply.

"All right, Miss Jenny. You can build your wall to suit yourself. But there'll be no hurry over it. Until the rains begin, Win and I'll sleep out in the open. We'll have to take turn about on watch at night, anyway. If we don't keep up a fire, some other spotted kitty will be sure to come nosing up the gully."

"There must also be lions in the vicinity," added Winthrope.

74

Miss Leslie said nothing until after the last pieces of meat had been handed around, and Blake sprang up to resume work.

"Mr. Blake," she called, in a low tone; "one moment, please. Would it save much bother if a door was made, and you and Mr. Winthrope should sleep inside?"

"We'll see about that later," replied Blake, carelessly.

The girl bit her lip, and the tears started to her eyes. Even Winthrope had started off without expressing his appreciation. Yet he at least should have realized how much it had cost her to make such an offer.

By evening she had her tree-cave–house, she preferred to name it to herself–in a habitable condition. When the purifying fire had burnt itself out, leaving the place free from all odors other than the wholesome smell of wood smoke, she had asked Blake how she could rake out the ashes. His advice was to wet them down where they lay.

This was easier said than done. Fortunately, the spring was only a few yards distant, and after many trips, with her palm-leaf hat for bowl, the girl carried enough water to sprinkle all the powdery ashes. Over them she strewed the leaves and grass which she had gathered while the fire was burning. The driest of the grass, arranged in a far corner, promised a more comfortable bed than had been her lot for the last three nights.

During this work she had been careful not to forget the fire at the tree. Yet when, near sundown, she called the others to the third meal of leopard meat, Blake grumbled at the tree for being what he termed such a confounded tough proposition.

"Good thing there's lots of wood here, Win," he added. "We'll keep this fire going till the blamed thing topples over, if it takes a year."

"Oh, but you surely will not stay so far from the baobab to-night!" exclaimed Miss Leslie.

"Hold hard!" soothed Blake. "You've no license to get the jumps yet a while. We'll have another fire by the baobab. So you needn't worry."

A few minutes later they went back to the baobab, and Winthrope began helping Miss Leslie to construct a bamboo screen in the narrow entrance of the tree-cave, while Blake built the second fire.

As Winthrope was unable to tell time by the stars, Blake took the first watch. At sunset, following the engineer's advice, Winthrope lay down with his feet to the small watch-fire, and was asleep before twilight had deepened into night. Fagged out by the mental and bodily

75

stress of the day, he slept so soundly that it seemed to him he had hardly lost consciousness when he was roused by a rough hand on his forehead.

"What is it?" he mumbled.

"'Bout one o'clock," said Blake. "Wake up! I ran overtime, 'cause the morning watch is the toughest. But I can't keep 'wake any longer."

"I say, this is a beastly bore," remarked Winthrope, sitting up.

"Um-m," grunted Blake, who was already on his back.

Winthrope rubbed his eyes, rose wearily, and drew a blazing stick from the fire. With this upraised as a torch, he peered around into the darkness, and advanced towards the spring.

When, having satisfied his thirst, he returned somewhat hurriedly to the fire, he was startled by the sight of a pale face gazing at him from between the leaves of the bamboo screen.

"My dear Miss Genevieve, what is the matter?" he exclaimed.

"Hush! Is he asleep?"

"Like a top."

"Thank Heaven! . . . . Good-night."

"Good-night—er—I say, Miss Genevieve—"

But the girl disappeared, and Winthrope, after a glance at Blake's placid face, hurried along the cleft to stack the other fire. When he returned he noticed two bamboo rods which Blake had begun to shape into bow staves. He looked them over, with a sneer at Blake's seemingly unskilful workmanship; but he made no attempt to finish the bows.

CHAPTER XI

A DESPOILED WARDROBE

Soon after sunrise Miss Leslie was awakened by the snap and dull crash of a falling tree. She made a hasty toilet, and ran out around the baobab. The burned tree, eaten half through by the fire, had been pushed over against the cliff by Blake and Winthrope. Both had already climbed up, and now stood on the edge of the cliff.

"Hello, Miss Jenny!" shouted Blake. "We've got here at last. Want to come up?"

"Not now, thank you."

"It's easy enough. But you're right. Try your hand again at the cutlets, won't you? While they're frying, we'll get some eggs for dessert How does that strike you?"

"We have no way to cook them."

"Roast 'em in the ashes. So long!"

Miss Leslie cooked breakfast over the watch-fire, for the other had been scattered and stamped out by the men when the tree fell. They came back in good time, walking carefully, that they might not break the eggs with which their pockets bulged. Between them, they had brought a round dozen and a half. Blake promptly began stowing all in the hot ashes, while Winthrope related their little adventure with unwonted enthusiasm.

"You should have come with us, Miss Genevieve," he began. "This time of day it is glorious on the cliff top. Though the rock is bare, there is a fine view—"

"Fine view of grub near the end," interpolated Blake.

"Ah, yes; the birds—you must take a look at them, Miss Genevieve! The sea end of the cliff is alive with them—hundreds and thousands, all huddled together and fighting for room. They are a sight, I assure you! They're plucky, too. It was well we took sticks with us. As it was, one of the gannets—boobies, Blake calls them—caught me a nasty nip when I went to lift her off the nest."

"Best way is to kick them off," explained Blake. "But the point is that we've hopped over the starvation stile. Understand? The whole blessed cliff end is an omelette waiting for our pan. Pass the leopardettes, Miss Jenny."

When the last bit of meat had disappeared, Blake raked the eggs from the ashes, and began to crack them, solemnly sniffing at each

77

before he laid it on its leaf platter. Some were a trifle "high." None, however, were thrown away.

When it was all over, Winthrope contemplated the scattered shells with a satisfied air.

"Do you know," he remarked, "this is the first time I have felt—er—replenished since we found those cocoanuts."

"How about one of 'em now to top off on?" questioned Blake.

Miss Leslie sighed. "Why did you speak of them! I am still hungry enough to eat more eggs—a dozen—that is, if we had a little salt and butter."

"And a silver cup and napkins!" added Blake. "About the salt, though, we'll have to get some before long, and some kind of vegetable food. It won't do to keep up this whole meat menu."

"If only those little bamboo sprouts were as good as they look—like a kind of asparagus!" murmured Miss Leslie.

"I've heard that the Chinese eat them," said Winthrope.

"They eat rats, too," commented Blake.

"We might at least try them," persisted Miss Leslie.

"How? Raw?"

"I have heard papa tell of roasting corn when he was a boy."

"That's so; and roasting-ears are better than boiled. Win, I guess we'll have a sample of bamboo asparagus *à la* Les-lee!"

Winthrope took the penknife, and fetched a handful of young sprouts from the bamboo thicket. They were heated over the coals on a grill of green branches, and devoured half raw.

"Say," mumbled Blake, as he ruminated on the last shoot, "we're getting on some for this smell hole of a coast: house and chicken ranch, and vegetables in our front yard— We've got old Bobbie Crusoe beat, hands down, on the start-off, and he with his shipful of stuff for handicap!"

"Then you believe that the situation looks more hopeful, Mr. Blake?"

"Well, we've at least got an extension on our note for a week or two. But I'm not going to coddle you with a lot of lies, Miss Jenny. There's the fever coming, sure as fate. I may stave it off a while; you and Win, ten to one, will be down in a few days—and not a smell of quinine in our commissary. Then there'll be dysentery and snakes and wild beasts—No; we're not out of the woods yet, not by a—considerable."

"By Jove, Blake," muttered Winthrope, "I must say, you're not very encouraging."

"Didn't say I was trying to be."

"But, Mr. Blake, I am sure papa will offer a large reward when the steamer is reported as lost. There will be ships searching for us—"

"We're not in the British Channel, and I'll bet what few boats do coast along here don't nose about much among these coral reefs."

"I fancy it would do no harm to erect a signal," said Winthrope.

"Only thing that would make a show is Miss Leslie's skirt," replied Blake.

"There is the big leopard skin," persisted Winthrope. To his surprise the engineer took the suggestion under serious consideration.

"Well, I don't know," he said. "If we had a water background, now. But against the rock and trees,—no; what we want is white. I'll tell you—when Miss Jenny sets to and makes herself a dress of that skin, I'll fly her skirt to the zephyrs."

"Mr. Blake! I really think that is cruel of you!"

"Oh, come now; that's not fair! I wouldn't have said a word, but you said you wanted to help."

"I beg your pardon, Mr. Blake. I—I did not quite understand you. I really do want to help—to do my share—"

"Now you're talking! You see, it's not only a question of the signal, but of clothes. We've got to figure anyway on needing new ones before long. Look at my pants and vest, and Win's too. Inside a month we'll all be in hide—or in hiding. That's a joke, Win, me b'y; see?"

"But in the meantime—" began Miss Leslie.

"In the meantime we're like to miss a chance or two of being picked up, just because we've failed to stick out a signal that'd catch the eye twice as far off as any other color than scarlet. Do you suppose I worked my way up from axeman to engineer, and didn't learn anything about flags?"

"But it is all really too absurd! I do not know the first thing about sewing, and I have neither thread nor needle."

"It's up to you, though, if you want to help. My sisters sewed mighty soon after they learned to toddle. 'Bout time you learned— There, now; I didn't mean to hurt your feelings. You've made a fair stagger at cooking, and I bet you win out on the dressmaking. For needle you can use one of these long slim thorns—poke a hole, and then slip the thread through, like a shoemaker."

"Ah, yes; but the thread?" put in Winthrope.

"The cocoanut fibre would hardly do," said Miss Leslie, forgetting to dry her eyes.

"No. We could get fairly good fibres out of the palm leaves; but catgut will be a whole lot better. I'll slit up a lot for you, fine enough to sew with. And now, let's get down to tacks. No offence—but did either of you ever learn to do anything useful in all your blessed little lives?"

"Why, Mr. Blake, of course I—"

"Of course what?" demanded Blake, as Miss Leslie hesitated. "We know all about your cooking and sewing. What else?"

"I—I see what you meant. I fear that nothing of what I learned would be of service now."

"Boarding-school rot, eh? And you, Winthrope?"

"If you would kindly name over what you have in mind."

"Um!" grunted Blake. "Well, it's first of all a question of a practical—practical, mind you,—knowledge of metallurgy, ceramics, and how to stick an arrow through a beef roast."

"I—ah—I believe I intimated that I have some knowledge of archery. But I doubt—"

"Cut it out! You'll have enough else to do. Get busy over those bows and arrows, and don't quit till you've got them in shape. Leave my bow good and stiff. I can pull like a mule can kick. Well, Miss Jenny; what is it?"

"Is not—has not ceramics something to do with burning china?"

"Sure!—china, pottery, and all that. Know anything about it?"

"Why, I have a friend who amuses herself by painting china, and I know it has to be burned."

"And that's all!" grunted Blake. "Well, let me tell you. When I was a little kid I used to work in a pottery. All I can remember is that they'd take clay, shape it into a pot, dry it, and bake the thing in a kiln. We've got to work the same game somehow. This kind of eating will mean dysentery in short order. So there's going to be a bean-pot for our stews, or Tom Blake'll know the reason why. Nurse up that ankle of yours, Win. We'll trek it to-morrow—cocoanuts, and maybe something else. There's clay on the far bank of the river, and across from it I saw a streak that looked like brown hæmatite."

CHAPTER XII

SURVIVAL OF THE FITTEST

The next four days slipped by almost unheeded. Blake saw to it that not only himself but his companions had work to occupy every hour of daylight. When not engaged in cooking and fuel gathering, Miss Leslie was learning by painful experience the rudiments of dressmaking.

At the start she had all but ruined the beautiful skin of the mother leopard before Blake chanced to see her and took over the task of cutting it into shape for a skirt. But when it came to making a waist of the cub fur, he said that she would have to puzzle out the pattern from her other one. Between cooking three meals a day over an open fire, gathering several armfuls of wood, and making a dress with penknife, thorn, and catgut, the girl had little time to think of other matters than her work.

Winthrope had been gazetted as hunter in ordinary. His task was to keep Miss Leslie supplied with fresh eggs and each day to kill as many of the boobies and cormorants as he could skin and split for drying. Blake had changed his mind about taking him when he went for cocoanuts. Instead, he had gone alone on several trips, bringing three or four loads of nuts, then a little salt from the seashore, dirty but very welcome, and last of all a great lump of clay, wrapped in palm fronds.

With this clay he at once began experiments in the art of pottery. Having mixed and beaten a small quantity, he moulded it into little cups and bowls, and tried burning them over night in the watch-fire. A few came out without crack or flaw. Vastly elated by this success, he fashioned larger vessels from his clay, and within the week could brag of two pots suitable for cooking stews, and four large nondescript pieces which he called plates. What was more, all had a fairly good sand glaze, for he had been quick to observe a glaze on the bottoms of the first pots, and had reasoned out that it was due to the sand which had adhered while they stood drying in the sun.

He next turned his attention to metallurgy. The first move was to search the river bank for the brown bog iron ore which he believed he had seen from the farther side. After a dangerous and exhausting day's work in the mire and jungle, he came back with nothing more to show for his pains than an armful of creepers. Late in the afternoon, he had located the hæmatite, only to find it lying in a streak so thin that he could not hope to collect enough for practical purposes.

"Lucky we've got something to fall back on," he added, after telling of his failure. "Pass over those keys of yours, Win. Good! Now untangle those creepers. To-night we'll take turns knotting them up into some sort of a rope-ladder. I'm getting mighty weary of hoofing it all around the point every time I trot to the river. After this I'll go down the cliff at that end of the gully."

Winthrope, who had become very irritable and depressed during the last two days, turned on his heel, with the look of a fretful child.

To cover this undiplomatic rudeness, Miss Leslie spoke somewhat hurriedly. "But why should you return again to the river, Mr. Blake? I'm sure you are risking the fever; and there must be savage beasts in the jungle."

"That's my business," growled Blake. He paused a moment, and added, rather less ungraciously, "Well, if you care, it's this way—I'm going to keep on looking for ore. Give me a little iron ore, and we'll mighty soon have a lot of steel knives and arrow-heads that'll amount to something. How're we going to bag anything worth while with bamboo tips on our arrows? Those boar tusks are a fizzle."

"So you will continue to risk your life for us? I think that is very brave and generous, Mr. Blake!"

"How's that?" demanded Blake, not a little puzzled. He was fully conscious of the risk; but this was the first intimation he had received or conceived that his motives were other than selfish—"Um-m! So that's the ticket. Getting generous, eh?"

"Not getting—you *are* generous! When I think of all you have done for us! Had it not been for you, I am sure we should have died that first day ashore."

"Well, don't blame me. I couldn't have let a dog die that way; and then, a fellow needs a Man Friday for this sort of thing. As for you, I haven't always had the luck to be favored with ladies' company."

"Thank you, Mr. Blake. I quite appreciate the compliment. But now, I must put on supper."

Blake followed her graceful movements with an intentness which, in turn, drew Winthrope's attention to himself. The Englishman smiled in a disagreeable manner, and resumed his work on the bows, with the look of one mentally preoccupied. After supper he found occasion to spend some little time among the bamboos.

When at sunset Miss Leslie withdrew into the baobab, Winthrope somewhat officiously insisted upon helping her set up her screen in the entrance. As he did so, he took the opportunity to hand her a bamboo knife, and to draw her attention to several double-pointed bamboo stakes which he had hidden under the litter.

"What is it?" she asked, troubled by his furtive glance back at Blake.

"Merely precaution, you know," he whispered. "The ground in there is quite soft. It will be no trouble, I fancy, to put up the stakes, with their points inclined towards the entrance."

"But why—"

"Not so loud, Miss Genevieve! It struck me that if any one should seek to enter in the night, he would find these stakes deucedly unpleasant. Be careful how you handle them. As you see, the sharper points, which are to be set uppermost, run off into a razor edge. Put them up now, before it grows too dark. You know how ninepins are set—that shape. Good-night! You see, with these to guard the entrance, you need not be afraid to go to sleep at once."

"Thank you," she whispered, and began to thrust the stakes into the ground as he had directed.

He had not been mistaken. The vague doubts and fears which she already entertained would have kept her awake throughout the night, but thanks to the sense of security afforded by the sword-bayonets of her silent little sentries, the girl was soon able to calm herself, and was fast asleep long before Blake wakened Winthrope.

Immediately after breakfast, Blake—who had spent his watch in grinding the edges from a stone and experimenting with split and bent twigs—put Winthrope's keys in the fire, and began an attempt to shape them into a knife-blade. To heat the steel to the required temperature, he used a bamboo blowpipe, with his lungs for bellows.

Winthrope turned away with an indifferent bearing; but Miss Leslie found herself compelled to stop and admire his dexterous use of his rude tools.

One after another, the keys were welded together, end to end, in a narrow ribbon of steel. The thinnest one, however, was not fastened to the tip until it had been used to burn a groove in the edge of a rib, selected from among the bones which Miss Leslie had thrown out of the baobab. The last key was then fastened to the others; the blade ground sharp, tempered, and inserted in the groove. Finally, pieces of the key-ring were fitted in bands around the bone, through notches cut in the ends of the steel blade. The result was a bone-handled, bone-backed knife, with a narrow cutting edge of fine steel.

Long before it was finished Miss Leslie had been forced away by the requirements of her own work. In fact, Blake did not complete his task until late in the afternoon. At the end, he spent more than an hour grinding the handle into shape. When he came to show the completed knife to Miss Leslie, he was fairly aglow with justifiable pride.

"How's that for an Eskimo job?" he demanded. "Bunch of keys and a bone, eh?"

"You are certainly very ingenious, Mr. Blake!"

"Nixy! There's little of the inventor in my top piece—only some hustle and a good memory. I was up in Alaska, you know. Saw a sight of Eskimo work."

"Still, it is very skilfully done."

"That may be—Look out for the edge! It'd do to shave. No more bamboo splinters for me—dull when you hit a piece of bone. I'm ready now to skin a rhinoceros."

"If you can catch one!"

"Guess we could find enough of them around here, all right. But we'll start in on some of Win's sheep and cattle."

"Oh, do! One grows tired of eggs, and all these sea-birds are so tough and fishy, no matter how I cook them."

"We'll sneak down to the pool, and make a try with the bows this evening. I'll give odds, though, that we draw a blank. Win's got the aim, but no drive; I've got the drive, but no aim. Even if I hit an antelope, I don't think a bamboo-pointed arrow would bother him much."

"Don't the savages kill game without iron weapons?"

"Sure; but a lot have flint points, and a lot of others use poison. I know that the Apaches and some of those other Southern Indians used to fix their arrows with rattlesnake poison."

"How horrible!"

"Well, that depends on how you look at it. I guess they thought guns more horrible when they tackled the whites and got the daylight let through 'em. At any rate, they swapped arrows for rifles mighty quick, and any one who knows Apaches will tell you it wasn't because they thought bullets would do less damage."

"Yet the thought of poison—"

"Yes; but the thought of self-preservation! Sooner than starve, I'd poison every animal in Africa—and so would you."

84

"I–I–You put it in such a horrible way. One must consider others, animals as well as people; and yet–"

"Survival of the fittest. I've read some things, and I'm no fool, if I do say it myself. For instance, I'm the boss here, because I'm the fittest of our crowd in this environment; but back in what's called civilized parts, where the law lets a few shrewd fellows monopolize the means of production, a man like your father–"

"Mr. Blake, it is not my fault if papa's position in the business world–"

"Nor his, either–it's the cussed system! No; that's all right, Miss Jenny. I was only illustrating. Now, I take it, both you and Win would like to get rid of a boss like me, if you could get rid of Africa at the same time. As it is, though, I guess you'd rather have me for boss, and live, than be left all by your lonesomes, to starve."

"I–I'm sure there is no question of your leadership, Mr. Blake. We have both tried our best to do what you have asked of us."

" *You* have, at least. But I know. If a ship should come to-morrow, it'd be Blake to the back seat. 'Papa, give this–er–person a check for his services, while I chase off with Winnie, to get my look-in on 'Is Ri-yal 'Igh-ness.'"

Miss Leslie flushed crimson– "I'm sure, Mr. Blake–"

"Oh, don't let that worry you, Miss Jenny. It don't me. I couldn't be sore with you if I tried. Just the same, I know what it'll be like. I've rubbed elbows enough with snobs and big bugs to know what kind of consideration they give one of the mahsses–unless one of the mahsses has the drop on them. Hello, Win! What's kept you so late?"

"None of your business!" snapped Winthrope.

Miss Leslie glanced at him, even more puzzled and startled by this outbreak than she had been by Blake's strange talk. But if Blake was angered, he did not show it.

"Say, Win," he remarked gravely, "I was going to take you down to the pool after supper, on a try with the bows. But I guess you'd better stay close by the fire."

"Yes; it is time you gave a little consideration to those who deserve it," rejoined Winthrope, with a peevishness of tone and manner which surprised Miss Leslie. "I tell you, I'm tired of being treated like a dog."

"All right, all right, old man. Just draw up your chair, and get all the hot broth aboard you can stow," answered Blake, soothingly.

Winthrope sat down; but throughout the meal, he continued to complain over trifles with the peevishness of a spoiled child, until Miss Leslie blushed for him. Greatly to her astonishment, Blake endured the nagging without a sign of irritation, and in the end took his bow and arrows and went off down the cleft, with no more than a quiet reminder to Winthrope that he should keep near the fire.

When, shortly after dark, the engineer came groping his way back up the gorge, he was by no means so calm. Out of six shots, he had hit one antelope in the neck and another in the haunch; yet both animals had made off all the swifter for their wounds.

The noise of his approach awakened Winthrope, who turned over, and began to complain in a whining falsetto. Miss Leslie, who was peering out through the bars of her screen, looked to see Blake kick the prostrate man. His frown showed only too clearly that he was in a savage temper. To her astonishment, he spoke in a soothing tone until Winthrope again fell asleep. Then he quietly set about erecting a canopy of bamboos over the sleeper.

Just why he should build this was a puzzle to the girl. But when she caught a glimpse of Blake's altered expression, she drew a deep breath of relief, and picked her way around the edge of her bamboo stakes, to lie down without a trace of the fear which had been haunting her.

CHAPTER XIII

THE MARK OF THE BEAST

Morning found Winthrope more irritable and peevish than ever. Though he had not been called on watch by Blake until long after midnight, he had soon fallen asleep at his post and permitted the fire to die out. Shortly before dawn, Blake was roused by a pack of jackals, snarling and quarrelling over the half-dried seafowl. To charge upon the thieves and put them to flight with a few blows of his club took but a moment. Yet daylight showed more than half the drying frames empty.

Blake was staring glumly at them, with his broad back to Winthrope, when Miss Leslie appeared. The sudden cessation of Winthrope's complaints brought his companion around on the instant. The girl stood before him, clad from neck to foot in her leopard-skin dress.

"Well, I'll be—dashed!" he exclaimed, and he stood staring at her open-mouthed.

"I fear it will be warm. Do you think it becoming?" she asked, flushing, and turning as though to show the fit of the costume.

"Do I?" he echoed. "Miss Jenny, you're a peach!"

"Thank you," she said. "And here is the skirt. I have ripped it open. You see, it will make a fine flag."

"If it's put up. Seems a pity, though, to do that, when we're getting on so fine. What do you say to leaving it down, and starting a little colony of our own?"

Miss Leslie raised the skirt in her outstretched hands. Behind it her face became white as the cloth.

"Well?" demanded Blake soberly, though his eyes were twinkling.

"You forget the fever," she retorted mockingly, and Blake failed to catch the quaver beneath the light remark.

"Say, you've got me there!" he admitted. "Just pass over your flag, and scrape up some grub. I'll be breaking out a big bamboo. There are plenty of holes and loose stones on the cliff. We'll have the signal up before noon."

Miss Leslie murmured her thanks, and immediately set about the preparation of breakfast.

When Blake had the bamboo ready, with one edge of the broad piece of white duck lashed to it with catgut as high up as the tapering staff would bear, he called upon Winthrope to accompany him.

"You can go, too, Miss Jenny," he added. "You haven't been on the cliff yet, and you ought to celebrate the occasion."

"No, thank you," replied the girl. "I'm still unprepared to climb precipices, even though my costume is that of a savage."

"Savage? Great Scott! that leopard dress would win out against any set of Russian furs a-going, and I've heard they're considered all kinds of dog. Come on. I can swing you into the branches, and it's easy from there up."

"You will excuse me, please."

"Yes, you can go alone," interposed Winthrope. "I am indisposed this morning, and, what is more, I have had enough of your dictation."

"You have, have you?" growled Blake, his patience suddenly come to an end. "Well, let me tell you, Miss Leslie is a lady, and if she don't want to go, that settles it. But as for you, you'll go, if I have to kick you every step."

Winthrope cringed back, and broke into a childish whine. "Don't—don't do it, Blake—Oh, I say, Miss Genevieve, how can you stand by and see him abuse me like this?"

Blake was grinning as he turned to Miss Leslie. Her face was flushed and downcast with humiliation for her friend. It seemed incredible that a man of his breeding should betray such weakness. A quick change came over Blake's face.

"Look here," he muttered, "I guess I'm enough of a sport to know something about fair play. Win's coming down with the fever, and's no more to blame for doing the baby act than he'll be when he gets the delirium, and gabbles."

"I will thank you to attend to your own affairs," said Winthrope.

"You're entirely welcome. It's what I'm doing.— Do you understand, Miss Jenny?"

"Indeed, yes; and I wish to thank you. I have noticed how patient you have been—"

"Pardon me, Miss Leslie," rasped Winthrope. "Can you not see that for a fellow of this class to talk of fair play and patience is the height of impertinence? In England, now, such insufferable impudence—"

"That'll do," broke in Blake. "It's time for us to trot along."

"But, Mr. Blake, if he is ill—"

"Just the reason why he should keep moving. No more of your gab, Win! Give your jaw a lay-off, and try wiggling your legs instead."

Winthrope turned away, crimson with indignation. Blake paused only for a parting word with Miss Leslie. "If you want something to do, Miss Jenny, try making yourself a pair of moccasins out of the scraps of skin. You can't stay in this gully all the time. You've got to tramp around some, and those slippers must be about done for."

"They are still serviceable. Yet if you think—"

"You'll need good tough moccasins soon enough. Singe off the hair, and make soles of the thicker pieces. If you do a fair job, maybe I'll employ you as my cobbler, soon as I get the hide off one of those skittish antelope."

Miss Leslie nodded and smiled in response to his jesting tone. But as he swung away after Winthrope, she stood for some time wondering at herself. A few days since she knew she would have taken Blake's remark as an insult. Now she was puzzled to find herself rather pleased that he should so note her ability to be of service.

When she roused herself, and began singeing the hair from the odds and ends of leopard skin, she discovered a new sensation to add to her list of unpleasant experiences. But she did not pause until the last patch of hair crisped close to the half-cured surface of the hide. Fetching the penknife and her thorn and catgut from the baobab, she gathered the pieces of skin together, and walked along the cleft to the ladder-tree. There had been time enough for Blake and Winthrope to set up the signal, and she was curious to see how it looked.

She paused at the foot of the tree, and gazed up to where the withered crown lay crushed against the edge of the cliff. The height of the rocky wall made her hesitate; yet the men, in passing up and down, had so cleared away the twigs and leaves and broken the branches on the upper side of the trunk, that it offered a means of ascent far from difficult even for a young lady.

The one difficulty was to reach the lower branches. She could hardly touch them with her finger-tips. But her barbaric costume must have inspired her. She listened for a moment, and hearing no sound to indicate the return of the men, clasped the upper side of the trunk with her hands and knees, and made an energetic attempt to climb. The posture was far from dignified, but the girl's eyes sparkled with satisfaction as she found herself slowly mounting.

When, flushed and breathless, she gained a foothold among the branches, she looked down at the ground, and permitted herself a merry little giggle such as she had not indulged in since leaving boarding-school. She had actually climbed a tree! She would show Mr. Blake that she was not so helpless as he fancied.

At the thought, she clambered on up, finding that the branches made convenient steps. She did not look back, and the screen of tree-tops beneath saved her from any sense of giddiness. As her head came above the level of the cliff, she peered through the foliage, and saw the signal-flag far over near the end of the headland. The big piece of white duck stood out bravely against the blue sky, all the more conspicuous for the flocks of frightened seafowl which wheeled above and around it.

Surprised that she did not see the men, Miss Leslie started to draw herself up over the cliff edge. She heard Winthrope's voice a few yards away on her left. A sudden realization that the Englishman might consider her exploit ill-bred caused her to sink back out of sight.

She was hesitating whether to descend or to climb on up, when Winthrope's peevish whine was cut short by a loud and angry retort from Blake. Every word came to the girl's ears with the force of a blow.

"You do, do you? Well, I'd like to know where in hell you come in. She's not your sister, nor your mother, nor your aunt, and if she's your sweetheart, you've both been damned close-mouthed over it."

There was an irritable, rasping murmur from Winthrope, and again came Blake's loud retort.

"Look here, young man, don't you forget you called me a cad once before. I can stand a good deal from a sick man; but I'll give it to you straight, you'd better cut that out. Call me a brute or a savage, if that'll let off your steam; but, understand, I'm none of your English kinds."

Again Winthrope spoke, this time in a fretful whine.

Blake replied with less anger: "That's so; and I'm going to show you that I'm the real thing when it comes to being a sport. Give you my word, I'll make no move till you're through the fever and on your legs again. What I'll do then depends on my own sweet will, and don't you forget it. I'm not after her fortune. It's the lady herself that takes my fancy. Remember what I said to you when you called me a cad the other time. You had your turn aboard ship. Now I can do as I please; and that's what I'm going to do, if I have to kick you over the cliff end first, to shut off your pesky interference."

The girl crouched back into the withered foliage, dazed with terror. Again she heard Blake speak. He had dropped into a bitter sneer.

"No chance? It's no nerve, you mean. You could brain me, easy enough, any night—just walk up with a club when I'm asleep. Trouble is, you're like most other under dogs—'fraid that if you licked your boss, there'd be no soup bones. So I guess I'm slated to stay boss of this colony—grand Poo Bah and Mikado, all in one. Understand? You mind your own business, and don't go to interfering with me any more! . . . . Now, if you've stared enough at the lady's skirt—"

The threat of discovery stung the girl to instant action. With almost frantic haste, she scrambled down to the lower branches, and sprang to the ground. She had never ventured such a leap even in childhood. She struck lightly but without proper balance, and pitched over sideways. Her hands chanced to alight upon the remnants of leopard skin. Great as was her fear, she stopped to gather all together in the edge of her skirt before darting up the cleft.

At the baobab she turned and gazed back along the cliff edge. Before she had time to draw a second breath, she caught a glimpse of Blake's palm-leaf hat, near the crown of the ladder tree.

"O-o-h!—he didn't see me!" she murmured. Her frantic strength vanished, and a deathly sickness came upon her. She felt herself going, and sought to kneel to ease the fall.

She was roused from the swoon by Blake's resonant shout: "Hey, Miss Jenny! where are you? We've got your laundry on the pole in fine shape!"

The girl's flaccid limbs grew tense, and her body quivered with a shudder of dread and loathing. Yet she set her little white teeth, and forced herself to rise and go out to face the men. Both met her look with a blank stare of consternation.

"What is it, Miss Genevieve?" cried Winthrope. "You're white as chalk!"

"It's the fever!" growled Blake. "She's in the cold stage. Get a pot on. We'll—"

"No, no; it's not that! It's only—I've been frightened!"

"Frightened?"

"By a—a dreadful beast!"

"Beast!" repeated Blake, and his pale eyes flashed as he sprang across to where his bow and arrows and his club leaned against the baobab. "I'll have no beasts nosing around my dooryard! Must be that skulking lion I heard last night. I'll show him!" He caught up his weapons and stalked off down the cleft.

"By Jove!" exclaimed Winthrope; "the man really must be mad. Call him back, Miss Genevieve. If anything should happen to him—"

"If only there might!" gasped the girl.

"Why, what do you mean?"

She burst into a hysterical laugh. "Oh! oh! it's such a joke–such a joke! At least he's not a hyena–oh, no; a brave beast! Hear him shout! And he actually thinks it's a lion! But it isn't–it's himself! Oh, dear! oh, dear! what shall I do?"

"Miss Genevieve, what do you mean? Be calm, pray, be calm!"

"Calm!–when I heard what he said? Yes; I heard every word! In the top of the tree–"

"In the tree? Heavens! Miss–er–Miss Genevieve!" stammered Winthrope, his face paling. "Did you–did you hear all?"

"Everything–everything he said! What shall I do? I am so frightened! What shall I do?"

"Everything *he* said?" echoed Winthrope.

"You spoke too low for me to hear; but I'm sure you faced him like a gentleman–I must believe it of you–"

Winthrope drew in a deep breath. "Ah, yes; I did, Miss Genevieve–I assure you. The beast! Yet you see the plight I am in. It is a nasty muddle–indeed it is! But what can I do? He is strong as a gorilla. Really, there is only one way–no doubt you heard him taunt me over it. I assure you I should not be afraid–but it would be so horrid–so cold-blooded. As a gentleman, you know–"

"No; it is not that!" broke in the girl. "He is right. Neither of us has the courage–even when he is asleep."

"My dear Miss Genevieve, this beast instinct to kill–"

"Yes; but think of him. If he is a beast, he is at least a brave one. While we–we haven't the courage of rabbits. I thought you called yourself an English gentleman. Are you going to stand by, and not lift a finger?"

"Really, now, Miss Genevieve, to murder a man–"

"Self-defence is not a crime–self-preservation. If you have a spark of manhood–"

"My dear–"

"For Heaven's sake, if you can't do anything, at least keep still! Oh, I'm sure I shall go mad! If only I had been drowned!"

"Ah, yes, to be sure. But really now, what you ask is a good deal for a man to risk. The fellow might wake up and murder me! Should I take the risk, might I–er–expect some manifestation of your gratitude, Miss Genevieve?"

"Of course! of course! I should always–"

"I–ah–refer to the–the–bestowal of your hand."

"My hand? I– Would you bargain for my esteem? I thought you a gentleman!"

"To be sure–to be sure! Who says I am not? But all is fair in love and war, you know. Your choice is quite free. I take it, you will not consider his–er–proposals. But if you do not wish my aid, you have another way of escape–that is–at least other women have done it."

The girl gazed at him, her eyes dilating with horror as she realized his meaning.

"No, no; not that!" she gasped. "I want to live–I've a right to live! Why, I'm only just twenty-two–I–"

"Hush!" cautioned Winthrope. "He's coming back. Be calm! There will be time until I get over this vile malaria. It may be that he himself will have the fever."

"He will not have the fever," replied the girl, in a hopeless tone, and she leaned back listlessly against the baobab, as Blake swung himself up, frowning and sullen, and flung his weapons from him.

"Bah!" he grumbled, "I told you that brute was a sneak. I've chased clean down to the pool and into the open, and not a smell of him. Must have hiked off into the tall grass the minute he heard me."

"If only he had gone off for good!" murmured Miss Leslie.

"Maybe he has; though you never can count on a sneak. Even you might be able to shoo him off next time; but, like as not, he'd come along when we were all out calling, and clean out our commissary. Guess I'll set to and run up a barricade down there where the gully is narrowest. There're shoals of dead thorn-brush to the right of the pool."

"Ah, yes; I fancy the vultures will be so vexed when they find your hedge in the way," remarked Winthrope.

"My! how smart we're getting!" retorted Blake. "Don't worry, though. We'll stow the stuff in Miss Jenny's boudoir, and I guess the birdies'll be polite enough to keep out."

"I must say, Blake, I do not see why you should wish to drag us away from here."

"There're lots of things you don't see, Win, me b'y–jokes, for instance. But what could you expect?–you're English. Now, don't get mad. Worst thing in the world for malaria."

"One would fancy you could see that I am not angry. I've a splitting headache, and my back hurts. I am ill."

Blake looked him over critically, and nodded. "That's no lie, old man. You're entitled to a hospital check all right. Miss Jenny, we'll

93

appoint you chief nurse. Make him comfortable as you can, and give him hot broth whenever he'll take it. You can do your sewing on the side. Whenever you need help, call on me. I'm going to begin that barricade."

CHAPTER XIV

FEVER AND FIRE AND FEAR

By nightfall Winthrope was tossing and groaning on the bed of leaves which Miss Leslie had heaped beneath his canopy. Though not delirious, his high temperature, coupled with the pains which racked every nerve and bone in his body, rendered him light-headed. He would catch himself up in the midst of some rambling nonsense to inquire anxiously whether he had said anything silly or strange. On being reassured upon this, he would relax again, and, as likely as not, break into a babyish wail over his aches and pains.

Blake shook his head when he learned that the attack had not been preceded by a chill.

"Guess he's in for a hot time," he said. "There is more'n one kind of malarial fever. Some are a whole lot like typhus."

"Typhus? What is that?" asked Miss Leslie.

"Sort of rapid fire, double action typhoid. Not that I think Win's got it—only malaria. What gets me is that we've only been here these few days, and yet it looks like he's got the continuous, no-chill kind."

"Then you think he will be very ill?"

"Well, I guess he'll think so. It ought to run out in a week or ten days, though. We've had good water, and it usually takes time for malaria to soak in deep. Now, don't worry, Miss Jenny. It'll do him no good, and you a lot of harm. Take things easy as you can, for you've got to keep up your strength. If you don't, you'll be down yourself before Win is up."

"Ill while he is helpless and unable—? Oh, no; that cannot be! I must not give way to the fever until—"

"Don't worry. You'll likely stave it off for a couple of weeks or so. You're lively yet, and that's a good sign. I knew Win was in for it when he began to grouch and loaf and do the baby act. I haven't much use for dudes in general, and English dudes in particular; but I'll admit that, while Win's soft enough in spots, he's not all mush and milk."

"Thank you, Mr. Blake."

"You're welcome. I couldn't say less, seeing that Win can't speak for himself. Now you tumble in and get a good sleep. I'll go on as night nurse, and work at the barricade same time. You're not going to do any night-nursing. I can gather the thorn-brush in the afternoons, and pile it up at night."

In the morning Miss Leslie found that Blake had built a substantial canopy over the invalid, in place of the first ramshackle structure.

"It's best for him to be out in the air," he explained; "so I fixed this up to keep off the dew. But whenever it rains, we'll have to tote him inside."

"Ah, yes; to be sure. How is he?" murmured the girl.

"He's about the same this morning. But he got a little sleep. Keep him dosed with all the hot broth he'll take. And say, roust me out at noon. I've had my breakfast. Now I'll have a snooze. So long!"

He nodded, and crawled under the shade of the nearest bush, too drowsy to observe her look of dismay.

At noon, having learned that Winthrope's condition showed little change, Blake ate a hearty meal, and at once set off down the cleft. He did not reappear until nightfall; though at intervals Miss Leslie had heard his step as he came up the ravine with his loads of thorn-brush.

This course of action became the routine for the following ten days. It was broken only by three incidents, all relating to the important matter of food supply. Winthrope had soon tired of broth, and showed such an insatiable craving for cocoanut milk that the stock on hand had become exhausted within the week.

The day after, Blake took the rope ladder, as he called the tangle of knotted creepers, and went off towards the north end of the cleft. When he returned, a little before dark, the lower part of his trousers was torn to shreds, and the palms of his hands were blistered and raw; but he carried a heavy load of cocoanuts. After a vain attempt to climb the giant palms on the far side of the river, he had found another grove near at hand, in the little plain, and had succeeded in reaching the tops of two of the smaller palms.

Under his directions, Miss Leslie clarified a bowl of bird fat—goose-grease, Blake called it,—and dressed his hands. Yet even with the bandages which she made of soft inner bark and the handkerchiefs, he was unable to handle the thorn-brush the following day. Unfortunately for him, he was not content to sit idle. During the night he had cut a bamboo fishing-pole and lengthened Miss Leslie's line of plaited cocoanut-fibre with a long catgut leader. In the afternoon he completed his outfit with a hairpin hook and a piece of half-dried meat.

He was back an hour earlier than usual, and he brought with him a dozen or more fair-sized fish. His mouth was watering over the prospective feast, and Miss Leslie showed herself hardly less eager for a change from their monotonous diet. As the fish were already dressed, she raked up the coals and quickly contrived a grill of green bamboos.

When the odor of the broiling fish spread about in the still air, even Winthrope sniffed and turned over, while Blake watched the crisping delicacies with a ravenous look. Unable to restrain himself, he caught up the smallest fish, half cooked, and bolted it down with such haste that he burnt his mouth. He ran over to the spring for a drink, and Winthrope cackled derisively.

Miss Leslie was too absorbed in her cooking to observe the result of Blake's greediness. She had turned the fish for the last time, and was about to lift them off the fire, when Blake came running back, and sent grill and all flying with a violent kick.

"Salt!" he gasped–"where's the salt? I'm poisoned!"

"Poisoned?"

"Poison fish! Don't eat! God!–Where's the salt?"

The girl stared at him. His agony was so great that beads of sweat were rolling down his face. He writhed, and stretched out a quivering hand–"Salt, quick!–warm water–salt!"

"But there's none left! You remember, yesterday–"

"God!" groaned Blake, and for a moment he sank down, overcome by a racking convulsion. Then his jaw closed like a bulldog's, and gritting his teeth with the effort, he staggered up and rushed off down the cleft.

"Stop! stop, Mr. Blake! Where are you going?" screamed the girl.

She started to run after him, but was halted by an outburst of delirious laughter. Winthrope was sitting upright and waving his fever-blotched hands–"Hi, hi! look at 'im run! 'E's got w'at'll do for 'im! Run, you swine; you–"

There followed a torrent of cockney abuse so foul that Miss Leslie blushed scarlet with shame as she sought to quiet him. But the excitement had so heightened his fever that he was in a raving delirium. It was close upon midnight before his temperature fell, and he sank into a death-like torpor. In her ignorance, she supposed that he had fallen asleep.

Her relief was short-lived, for soon she remembered Blake. She could see him lying beside the pool or out on the bare plain, his resolute eyes cold and glassy, his powerful body contorted in the death agony. The vision filled her with dismay. With all his coarseness, the man had showed himself so resourceful, so indomitable, that when she sought to dwell upon her reasons to fear him, she found herself admiring his virile manliness. He might be a brute, but he did not belong among the jackals and hyenas. Indeed, as she called to mind his strong face and frank, blunt speech she all but disbelieved what her own ears had heard.

And anyway, without his aid, what should she do? Winthrope had already become as weak as a child. The emaciation of his jaundiced features was a mockery of their former plumpness. Blake had said that the fever might run on for another week, and that even if Winthrope recovered, he would probably be helpless for several days besides.

What was no less serious, though she had concealed the fact from Blake, she herself had been troubled the past week with the depression and lassitude which had preceded Winthrope's attack. If Blake was dead, and she should fall ill before Winthrope recovered, they would both die from lack of care. And if they did not die of the fever, what of their future, here on this desolate savage coast!

But the very keenness of her mental anguish so exhausted and numbed the girl's brain that she at last fell into a heavy sleep. The fire burned low, and shadowy forms began to creep from behind the bamboos and the trees and rocks down the gorge. There was no sound; but greedy, wolfish eyes gleamed in the starlight.

Only the day before Blake had told Miss Leslie to store the last rack of cured meat inside the baobab. The two sleepers lay between the fire and the entrance to the hollow. Slowly the embers of the fire died away into gray ashes, and slowly the night prowlers drew nearer. The boldest of the pack crept close to Miss Leslie, and, with teeth bared and back bristling, sniffed at the edge of her skirt. Whether because of her heavy breathing or the odor of the leopard skin, the beast drew away, with an uneasy whine.

There was a pause; then, backed by three others, the leader approached Winthrope. He was still lying in the death-like torpor, and he lacked the protection which, in all likelihood, the leopard skin had given Miss Leslie. The cowardly brutes took him for dead or dying. They sniffed at him from head to foot, and then, with a ferocious outburst of snarls and yells, flung themselves upon him.

Had it not chanced that Winthrope was lying upon his side, with one arm thrown up, he would have been fatally wounded by the first slashing bites of his assailants. The two which sought to tear him were baffled by the thick folds of Blake's coat, while their leader's slash at the victim's throat was barred by the upraised arm. With a savage snap, the beast's jaws closed on the arm, biting through to the bone. At the same instant the fourth jackal tore ravenously at one of the outstretched legs.

98

With a shriek of agony, Winthrope started up from his torpor, and struck out frantically in a fury of pain and terror. Startled by the violence of this unexpected resistance, the jackals leaped back—only to spring in again as the remainder of the pack made a rush to forestall them.

Winthrope was staggering to his feet, when the foremost brute leaped upon him. He fell heavily against one of the main supports of his bamboo canopy, and the entire structure came down with a crash. Two of the jackals, caught beneath the roof, howled with fear as they sought to free themselves. The others, with brute dread of an unknown danger, drew away, snarling and gnashing their teeth.

Wakened by the first ferocious yelps of Winthrope's assailants, Miss Leslie had started up and stared about in the darkness. On all sides she could see pairs of fiery eyes and dim forms like the phantom creatures of a nightmare. Winthrope's shriek, instead of spurring her to action, only confused her the more and benumbed her faculties. She thought it was his death cry, and stood trembling, transfixed with horror.

Then came the fall of the canopy. His cries as he sought to throw it off showed that he was still alive. In a flash her bewilderment vanished. The stagnant blood surged again through her arteries in a fiery, stimulating torrent. With a cry, to which primeval instinct lent a menacing note, she groped her way to the fallen canopy, and stooped to lift up one side.

"Quick!—into the tree!" she called.

Still frantic with terror, Winthrope struggled to his feet. She thrust him towards the baobab, and followed, dragging the mass of interwoven bamboos. Emboldened by the retreat of their quarry, the snarling pack instantly began to close in. Fortunately they were too cowardly to rush at once, and fear spurred their intended victims to the utmost haste. Groping and stumbling, the two felt their way to the baobab, and Miss Leslie pushed Winthrope headlong through the entrance. As he fell, she turned to face the pack.

The foremost beasts were at the rear edge of the bamboo framework, their eyes close to the ground. Instinct told her that they were crouching to leap. With desperate strength she caught up the canopy before her like a great shield, and drew it in after her until the ends of the cross-bars were wedged fast against the sides of the opening. Though it seemed so firm, she clung to it with a convulsive grasp as she felt the pack leaders fling themselves against the outer side.

But Blake had lashed the bamboos securely together, and none of the beasts was heavy enough to snap the supple bars. Finding that they could not break down the barrier, they began to scratch and tear at the thatch which covered the frame. Soon a pair of lean jaws thrust in and snapped at the girl's skirt. She sprang back, with a cry: "Help! Quick, Mr. Winthrope! They're breaking through!"

Winthrope made no response. She stooped, and found him lying inert where he had fallen. She had only herself to depend upon. A screen of sharp sticks which she had made for the entrance was leaning against the inner wall, within easy reach. To grasp it and thrust it against the other framework was the work of an instant.

Still she trembled, for the eager beasts had ripped the thatch from the canopy, and their inthrust jaws made short work of the few leaves on her screen. Unaware that even a lion or a tiger is quickly discouraged by the knife-like splinters of broken bamboo, she expected every moment that the jackals would bite their way through her frail barrier.

She remembered the stakes given her by Winthrope, hidden under the leaves and grass of her bed. She groped her way across the hollow, and uncovered one of the stakes. In her haste she cut her hand on its razor-like edge. All unheeding, she sprang back towards the entrance. She was none too soon. One of the smaller jackals had forced its head and one leg between the bars, and was struggling to enlarge the opening.

Fearful that the whole pack was about to burst in upon her, the girl grasped the bamboo stake in both hands, and began stabbing and lunging at the beast with all her strength. The jackal squirmed and snarled and snapped viciously. But the girl was now frantic. She pressed nearer, and though the white teeth grazed her wrist, she drove home a thrust that changed the beast's snarls into a howl of pain. Before she could strike again, it had struggled back out of the hole, beyond reach.

Tense and panting with excitement, she leaned forward, ready to stab at the next beast. None appeared, and presently she became aware that the pack had been daunted by the experience of their unlucky fellow. Their snarls and yells had subsided to whines, which seemed to be coming from a greater distance. Still she waited, with the bamboo stake upraised ready to strike, every nerve and muscle of her body tense with the strain.

So great was the stress of her fear and excitement that she had not heeded the first gray lessening of the night. But now the glorious tropical dawn came streaming out of the east in all its red effulgence.

Above and through the bamboo barrier glowed a light such as might have come from a great fire on the cliff top. Still tense and immovable, the girl stared out up the cleft. There was not a jackal in sight. She leaned forward and peered around, unable to believe such good fortune. But the night prowlers had slunk off in the first gray dawn.

The girl drew in a deep, shuddering sigh, and sank back. Her hand struck against Winthrope's foot. She turned about quickly and looked at him. He was lying upon his face. She hastened to turn him upon his side, and to feel his forehead. It was cool and moist. He was fast asleep and drenched with sweat. The great shock of his pain and fear and excitement had broken his fever.

With the relief and joy of this discovery, the girl completely relaxed. Not observing Winthrope's wounds, which had bled little, she sought to force a way out through the entrance. It was by no means an easy task to free the wedged framework, and when, after much pulling and pushing, she at last tore the mass loose, she found herself perspiring no less freely than Winthrope.

She was far too preoccupied, however, to consider what this might mean. Her first thought was of the fire. She ran to her rude stone fireplace and raked over the ashes. They were still warm, but there was not a live ember among them. Yet she realized that Winthrope must have hot food when he wakened, and Blake had carried with him the magnifying glass. For a little she stood hesitating. But the defeat of the jackals had given her courage and resolution such as she had never before known. She returned into the cave, and chose the sharpest of her stakes. Having made certain that Winthrope was still asleep, she set off boldly down the cleft.

At the first turn she came upon Blake's thorn barricade. It stretched across the narrowest part of the cleft in an impenetrable wall, twelve feet high. Only in the centre was a gap, which could have been filled by Blake in less than two hours' work. The girl's eyes brightened. She herself could gather the thorn-brush and fill the gap before night. They no longer need fear the jackals or even the larger beasts of prey. None the less, they must have fire.

Spurred on by the thought, she was about to spring through the barricade when she heard the tread of feet on the path beyond. She crouched down, and peered through the tangle of brush in the edge of the gap. Less than ten paces away Blake was plodding heavily up the trail. She stepped out before him.

"You—you! Are you alive?" she gasped.

101

"'Live? You bet your boots!" came back the grim response. "You bet I'm alive—though I had to go Jonah one better to do it. The whale heaved him up; I heaved up the whale—and it took about a barrel of sea-water to do it."

"Sea-water?"

"Sure . . . . I tumbled over twice on the way. But I made the beach. Lord! how I pumped in the briny deep! Guess I won't go into details— but if you think you know anything about seasickness— *Whew!* Lucky for yours truly, the tide was just starting out, and the wind off shore. I'd fallen in the water, and the Jonah business laid me out cold. Didn't know anything until the tide came up again and soused me."

"I am very glad you're not dead. But how you must have suffered! You are still white, and your face is all creased."

Blake attempted a careless laugh. "Don't worry about me. I'm here, O. K., all that's left,—a little wobbly on my pins, but hungry as a shark. But say, what's up with you? You're sweating like a— Good thing, though. It'll stave off your spell of fever a while. How 'd you happen to be coming down here so early?"

"I was starting to find you."

"Me!"

"Not you—that is, I thought you were dead. I was going to make certain, and to—to get the burning-glass."

"Um-m. I see. Let the fire go out, eh?"

"Do not blame me, Mr. Blake! I was so ill and worn out, and I've paid for it twice over, really I have. Didn't those awful beasts attack you?"

"Beasts? How's that?" he demanded.

"Oh, but you must have heard them! The horrid things tried to kill us!" she cried, and she poured out a half incoherent account of all that had happened since he left.

Blake listened intently, his jaw thrust out, his eyes glowing upon her with a look which she had never before seen in any man's eyes. But his first comment had nothing to do with her conduct.

"How's that?—sorry Win got rousted out of his nice little snooze— Snooze! Why, don't you know, we'd been all alone in our glory by to-night if it hadn't been for those brutes. He was in the stupor, and that would have been the end of him if the beasts hadn't stirred him up so lively. I've heard of such a thing before, but I always thought it was a fake. Here you are sweating, too."

"I feel much better than yesterday. I did not tell you, but I have felt ill for nearly a week."

"'Fraid to tell, eh?—and you were so scared over the beasts— Scared! By Jiminy, you've got grit, little woman! There's two kinds of scaredness; you've got the Stonewall Jackson kind. If anybody asks you, just refer them to Tommy Blake."

"Thank you, Mr. Blake. But should we not hasten back now to prepare something for Mr. Winthrope?"

"Ditto for yours truly. I'm like that sepulchre you read about— white outside, and within nothing but bare bones and emptiness."

CHAPTER XV

WITH BOW AND CLUB

The fire was soon re-lit, and a pot of meat set on to stew. It had ample time to simmer. Winthrope was wrapped in a life-giving sleep, out of which he did not waken until evening, while Blake, unable to wait for the pot to boil, and nauseated by the fishy odor of the dried seafowl, hunted out the jerked leopard meat, and having devoured enough to satisfy a native, fell asleep under a bush.

The sun was half down the sky when he sat up and looked around, wide awake the moment he opened his eyes. Miss Leslie was quietly placing an armful of sticks on the fuel heap beside the baobab.

"Hello, Miss Jenny! Hard at it, I see," he called cheerfully.

"Hush!" she cautioned. "Mr. Winthrope is still asleep."

"Good thing for him. He'll need all of that he can get."

"Then you think—?"

"Well, between you and me, I don't believe Win was built for the tropics. This fever of his, coming on so soon, wouldn't have hit nine men in ten half so hard. He's bound to have another spell in a month or two, and—"

"But cannot we possibly get away from here before then? Is there no way? Surely, you are so resourceful—"

"Nothing doing, Miss Jenny! Give me tools, and I'd engage to turn out a seagoing boat. But as it is, the only thing I could do would be to fire-burn a log. That would take two or three months, and in the end we'd have a lop-sided canoe that'd live about half a second in one of these tropic squalls."

"Do not the natives sail in canoes?"

"Maybe they do—and they make fire by rubbing sticks. We don't."

"But what can we do?"

"Take our medicine, and wait for a ship to show up."

"But we have no medicine."

"Have no— Say, Miss Jenny, you really ought to have stayed home from boarding-school and England long enough to learn your own language. I meant, we've got to take what's coming to us, without laying down or grouching. Both are the worst thing out for malaria."

"You mean that we must resign ourselves to this intolerable situation—that we must calmly sit here and wait until the fever—"

"No; I'll take care we don't sit around very much. We'll go on the hike, soon as Win can wobble. Which reminds me, I've got a little hike on hand now. I'm going to close up that barricade before dark. Me for a quiet night!"

Without waiting for a reply, he took his weapons, and swung briskly away down the cleft.

He returned a few minutes before sunset, with what appeared to be a large fur bag upon his back. Miss Leslie was pouring a bowl of broth from the stew-pot, and did not notice him until he sang out to her: "Hey, Miss Jenny, spill over that stuff! No more of that in ours!"

"It's for Mr. Winthrope. He has just wakened," she replied, still intent on her pouring.

"And you'd kill him with that slop! Heave it over. He's going to have beef juice."

"Oh! what's that on your back? You've killed an antelope!"

"Sure! Bushbuck, I guess they call him. Sneaked up when he was drinking, and stuck an arrow into his side. He jumped off a little way, and turned to see what'd bit him. I hauled off and put the second arrow right through his eye, into his brain. Neatest thing you ever saw."

"You surely are becoming a splendid archer!"

"Yes; Jim dandy! I could do it again about once in ten thousand shots. All the same, I've raked in this peacherino. Trot out your grill and we'll have something fit to eat."

"You spoke of beef juice."

"I've a dozen steaks ready to broil. Slap 'em on the fire, and I'll squeeze out enough juice with my fist to do Win for to-night."

He made good his assertion, using several of the steaks, which, having lost less than half their juices in the process, were eaten with great relish by Miss Leslie and himself.

Winthrope, after drinking the stimulating beef juice and a quantity of hot water, turned over and fell asleep again while Blake was dressing his wounds. None of these was serious of itself; but Blake knew the danger of infection in the tropics, and carefully washed out the gashes before applying the tallow salve which Miss Leslie had tried out from the antelope fat.

The dressing was completed by torchlight. Blake then rolled the sleeper into a comfortable position, took the torch from Miss Leslie, and left the cave, pausing at the entrance to mutter a gruff good-night. The girl murmured a response, but watched him anxiously as he passed out. A step beyond the entrance he paused and turned again. In the red

105

glare of the torch, his face took on an expression that filled her with fright. Shrouded by the gloom of the hollow, she drew back to her bed, and without turning her eyes away from him, groped for one of her bamboo stakes.

But before she could arm herself, she saw Blake stoop over and grasp with his free hand the mass of interwoven bamboos. He straightened himself, and the framework swung lightly up and over, until it stood on end across the cave entrance. The girl stole around and peered out at him. He had spread open the antelope skin, and was beginning to slice the meat for drying. Though his forehead was furrowed, his expression was by no means sinister. Relieved at the thought that the light must have deceived her, she returned to her bed and was soon sleeping as soundly as Winthrope.

Blake strung the greater part of the meat on the drying racks, built a smudge fire beneath, and stretched the antelope skin on a frame. This done, he took his club and a small piece of bloody meat, and walked stealthily down the cleft to the barricade. Quiet as was his approach, it was met by a warning yelp on the farther side of the thorny wall, and he could hear the scurry of fleeing animals.

He kept on until the barricade loomed up before him in the starlight. From cliff to cliff the wall now stretched across the gorge without hole or gap. But Blake grasped the trunk of a young date-palm which projected from the barricade near the bottom, and pushed it out. The displacement of the spiky fronds disclosed the low passage which he had made in the centre of the barricade. He placed the piece of meat on one side, two or three feet from the hole, and squatted down across from it, with his club balanced on his shoulder.

Half an hour passed—an hour; and still he waited, silent and motionless as a statue. At last stealthy footsteps sounded on the outer side of the thorn wall, and an animal began to creep through the wall, sniffing for the bait. Blake waited with the immobility of an Eskimo. The delay was brief.

With a boldness for which Blake had not been prepared, the beast leaped through and seized the meat. Even in the dim light, Blake could see that he had lured an animal larger than any jackal. But this only served to lend greater force to his blow. As he struck, he leaped to his feet The brute fell as though struck by lightning and lay still.

Blake prodded the inert form warily; then knelt and passed his hands over it. The beast had whirled about just in time to meet the descending club, and the blow had crushed in its skull. Chuckling at the

106

success of his ruse, he drew the palm back into the opening, and swung his prize over his shoulder. When he came to the fire, a glance showed him that he had killed a full-grown spotted hyena.

In the morning, when Miss Leslie appeared, there were two hides stretched on bamboo frames, and the air was dark with vultures streaming down into the cleft near the barricade. Blake was sleeping the sleep of the just, and did not waken until she had built the fire and begun to broil the steaks which he had saved.

Again they had a feast of the fresh antelope meat. But with repletion came more of fastidiousness, and Blake agreed with Miss Leslie when she remarked that salt would have added to the flavor. He set off presently, and spent half a day on the talus of the headland, gathering salt from the rock crannies.

For the next three days he left the cleft only to gather eggs. The greater part of his time was spent in tanning the hyena and antelope skins. Meantime Miss Leslie continued to nurse Winthrope and to gather firewood. Under Blake's directions, she also purified the salt by dissolving it in a pot of water, and allowing the dirt to settle, when the clarified solution was poured off and evaporated over the fire in one of the earthenware pans.

At first Winthrope had been too weak to sit up. But treated to a liberal diet of antelope broth, raw eggs, hot water, and cocoanut milk, he gained strength faster than Blake had expected. On the fourth day Blake set him to work on the final rubbing of the new skins; on the fifth, he ordered him to go for eggs.

Much to Miss Leslie's surprise, Winthrope started off without a word of protest. All his peevish irritability and childishness had gone with the fever, and the girl was gratified to see the quiet manner in which he set about a task which seemed an imposition upon his half-regained strength. But the very motive which, seemingly, prevented him from protesting, impelled her to speak for him.

"Mr. Blake!" she exclaimed, "Mr. Winthrope is going off without a word; but I can't endure it! You have no right to send him on such an errand. It will kill him!"

Blake met her indignant look with a sober stare.

"What if it does!" he said. "Better for him to die in the gallant service of his fellows, than to sit here and rot. Eh, Win?"

"Do not trouble yourself, Miss Genevieve. I hope I shall pull through all right. If not—"

"No, you shall not! I'll go myself!"

"See here, Miss Leslie," said Blake, somewhat sternly; "who's got the responsibility of keeping you two alive for the next month or so? I've been in the tropics before, and I know something of the way people have to live to get out again. I'm trying to do my best, and I tell you straight, if you won't mind me, I'm going to make you, no matter how much it hurts your feelings. You see how nice and meek Win takes his orders. I explained matters to him last night—"

"I assure you, Blake, you shall have no cause for complaint as to my conduct," muttered Winthrope. "I should like to observe, however, that in speaking to Miss Leslie—"

"There you are again, with your everlasting talk. Cut it out, and get busy. To-morrow we all go on a hike to the river."

As Winthrope started off, Blake turned to Miss Leslie, with a good-natured grin.

"You see, it's this way, Miss Jenny—" he began. He caught her look of disdain, and his face darkened. "Mad, eh? So that's the racket!"

"Mr. Blake, I will not have you talk to me in that way. Mr. Winthrope is a gentleman, but nothing more to me than a friend such as any young woman—"

"That settles it! I'll take your word for it, Miss Jenny," broke in Blake, and springing up, he set about his work, whistling.

The girl gazed at his broad back and erect head, uncertain whether she should feel relieved or anxious. The more she thought the matter over, the more uncertain she became, and the more she wondered at her uncertainty. Could it be possible that she was becoming interested in a man who, if her ears had not deceived her— But no! That could not be possible!

Yet what a ring there was to his voice!—so clear and tonic after Winthrope's precise, modulated drawl. And her countryman's firmness! He could be rude if need be; but he would make her do what he thought was best for her health. Was it not possible that she had misunderstood his words on the cliff, and so misjudged—wronged—him?—that Winthrope, so eager to stipulate for her hand— But then Winthrope had more than confirmed her dreadful conclusions taken from Blake's words, and Winthrope was an English gentleman. It could not be possible that an English gentleman—

She ended in a state of utter bewilderment.

CHAPTER XVI

THE SAVAGE MANIFEST

As Winthrope had succeeded in dragging himself to and from the headland without a collapse, the following morning, as soon as the dew was dry, Blake called out all hands for the expedition. He was in the best of humors, and showed unexpected consideration by presenting Winthrope with a cane, which he had cut and trimmed during the night.

Having sent Miss Leslie to fill the whiskey flask with spring water, he dropped three cocoanut-shell bowls, a piece of meat and a lump of salt into one of the earthenware pots, and slung all over his shoulder in the antelope skin. With his bow hung over the other shoulder, knife and arrows in his belt, and his big club in hand, he looked ready for any contingency.

"We'll hit first for the mouth of the river," he said. "I'm going on ahead. If I'm not in sight when you come up, pick a tree where the ground is dry, and wait."

"But I say, Blake," replied Winthrope, "I see animals over in the coppices, and you should know that I am physically unable—"

"Nothing but antelope," interrupted Blake. "I've seen them enough now to know them twice as far off. And you can bet on it they'd not be there if any dangerous beast was in smelling distance."

"That is so clever of you, Mr. Blake," remarked Miss Leslie.

"Simple enough when you happen to think of it," responded Blake. "Yes; the only thing you've got to look out for's the ticks in the grass. They'll keep you interested. They bit me up in great shape."

He scowled at the recollection, nodded by way of emphasis, and was off like a shot. The edge of the plain beneath the cliff was strewn with rocks, among which, even with Miss Leslie's help, Winthrope could pick his way but slowly. Before they were clear of the rough ground, they saw Blake disappear among the mangroves.

The ticks proved less annoying than they had apprehended after Blake's warning. But when they approached the mouth of the river, they were alarmed to hear, above the roar of the surf, loud snorting, such as could only be made by large animals. Fearful lest Blake had roused and angered some forest beast, they veered to the right, and ran to hide behind a clump of thorns. Winthrope sank down exhausted the moment they reached cover; but Miss Leslie crept to the far end of the thicket and peered around.

"Oh, look here!" she cried. "It's a whole herd of elephants trying to cross the river mouth where we did, and they're being drowned, poor things!"

"Elephants?" panted Winthrope, and he dragged himself forward beside her. "Why, so there are; quite a drove of the beasts. Yet, I must say, they appear smaller–ah, yes; see their heads. They must be the hippos Blake saw."

"Those ugly creatures? I once saw some at the zoo. Just the same, they will be drowned. Some are right in the surf!"

"I can't say, I'm sure, Miss Genevieve, but I have an idea that the beasts are quite at home in the water. I fancy they enjoy surf bathing as keenly as ourselves."

"I do believe you are right. There is one going in from the quiet water. But look at those funny little ones on the backs of the others!"

"Must be the baby hippos," replied Winthrope, indifferently. "If you please, I'll take a pull at the flask. I am very dry."

When he had half emptied the flask, he stretched out in the shade to doze. But Miss Leslie continued to watch the movements of the snorting hippos, amused by the ponderous antics of the grown ones in the surf, and the comic appearance of the barrel-like infants as they mounted the backs of their obese mothers.

Presently Blake came out from among the mangroves, and walked across to the beach, a few yards away from the huge bathers. To all appearances, they paid as little attention to him as he to them. Miss Leslie glanced about at Winthrope. He was fast asleep. She waited a few moments to see if the hippopotami would attack Blake. They continued to ignore him, and gaining courage from their indifference, she stepped out from behind the thicket, and advanced to where Blake was crouched on the beach. When she came up, she saw beside him a heap of oysters, which he was opening in rapid succession.

"Hello! You're just in time to help," he called. "Where's Win?"

"Asleep behind those bushes."

"Worst thing he could do. But lend a hand, and we'll shuck these oysters before rousting him out. You can rinse those I've opened. Fill the pot with water, and put them in to soak."

"They look very tempting. How did you chance to find them?"

"Saw 'em on the mangrove roots at low tide, first time I nosed around here. Tide was well up to-day; but I managed to get these all right with a little diving. Only trouble, the skeets most ate me alive."

Miss Leslie glanced at her companion's dry clothing, and came back to the oysters themselves. "These look very tempting. Do you like them raw?"

"Can't say I like them much any way, as a rule. But if I did, I wouldn't eat this mess raw."

"Yes?"

"This must be the dry season here, and the river is running mighty clear. Just the same, it's nothing more than liquid malaria. We'll not eat these oysters till they've been pasteurized."

"If the water is so dangerous, I fear we will suffer before we can return," replied Miss Leslie, and she held up the flask.

"What!" exclaimed Blake. "Half gone already? That was Winthrope."

"He was very thirsty. Could we not boil a potful of the river water?"

"Yes, when the ebb gets strong, if we run too dry. First, though, we'll make a try for cocoanuts. Let's hit out for the nearest grove now. The main thing is to keep moving."

As he spoke, Blake caught up the pot and his club, and started for the thorn clump, leaving the skin, together with the meat and the salt, for Miss Leslie to carry. Winthrope was wakened by a touch of Blake's foot, and all three were soon walking away from the seashore, just within the shady border of the mangrove wood.

At the first fan-palm Blake stopped to gather a number of leaves, for their palm-leaf hats were now cracked and broken. A little farther on a ruddy antelope, with lyrate horns, leaped out of the bush before them and dashed off towards the river before Blake could string his bow. As if in mockery of his lack of readiness, a troupe of large green monkeys set up a wild chattering in a tree above the party.

"I say, Miss Jenny, do you think you can lug the pot, if we go slow? It isn't far now."

"I'll try."

"Good for you, little woman! That'll give me a chance to shoot quick."

They moved on again for a hundred yards or more; but though Blake kept a sharp lookout both above and below, he saw no game other than a few small birds and a pair of blue wood-pigeons. When he sought to creep up on the latter, they flew into the next tree. In following them, he came upon a conical mound of hard clay, nearly four feet high.

"Hello; this must be one of those white anthills," he said, and he gave the mound a kick.

Instantly a tiny object whirred up and struck him in the face.

"Whee!" he exclaimed, springing back and striking out. "A hornet! No; it's a bee!"

"Did it sting you?" cried Miss Leslie.

"Sting? Keep back; there's a lot more of 'em. Sting? Oh, no; he only hypodermicked me with a red-hot darning needle! Shy around here. There's a whole swarm of the little devils, and they're hopping mad. Hear 'em buzz!"

"But where is their hive?" asked Winthrope, as all three drew back behind the nearest bushes.

"Guess they've borrowed that ant-hill," replied Blake, gingerly fingering the white lump which marked the spot where the bee had struck him.

"Wouldn't it be delightful if we had some honey?" exclaimed Miss Leslie.

"By Jove, that really wouldn't be half bad!" chimed in Winthrope.

"Maybe we can, Miss Jenny; only we'll need a fire to tackle those buzzers. Guess it'll be as well to let them cool off a bit also. The cocoanuts are only a little way ahead now. Here; give me the pot."

They soon came to a small grove of cocoanut palms, where Blake threw down his club and bow and handed his burning-glass to Miss Leslie.

"Here," he said; "you and Win start a fire. It's early yet, but I'm thinking we'll all be ready enough for oyster stew."

"How about the meat?" asked Miss Leslie.

"Keep that till later. Here goes for our dessert."

Selecting one of the smaller palms, Blake spat on his hands, and began to climb the slender trunk. Aided by previous experiences, he mounted steadily to the top. The descent was made with even more care and steadiness, for he did not wish to tear the skin from his hands again.

"Now, Win," he said, as he neared the bottom and sprang down, "leave the cooking to Miss Leslie, and husk some of those nuts. You won't more'n have time to do it before the stew is ready."

Winthrope's response was to draw out his penknife. Blake stretched himself at ease in the shade, but kept a critical eye on his companions. Although Winthrope's fingers trembled with weakness, he worked with a precision and rapidity that drew a grunt of approval from Blake. Presently Miss Leslie, who had been stirring the stew with a twig, threw in a little salt, and drew the pot from the fire.

"*En avant*, gentlemen! Dinner is served," she called gayly.

"What's that?" demanded Blake. "Oh; sure. Hold on, Miss Jenny. You'll dump it all."

He wrapped a wisp of grass about the pot, and filled the three cocoanut bowls. The stew was boiling hot; but they fished up the oysters with the bamboo forks that Blake had carved some days since. By the time the oysters were eaten, the liquor in the bowl was cool enough to drink. The process was repeated until the pot had been emptied of its contents.

"Say, but that was something like," murmured Blake. "If only we'd had pretzels and beer to go with it! But these nuts won't be bad."

When they finished the cocoanuts, Winthrope asked for a drink of water.

"Would it not be best to keep it until later?" replied Miss Leslie.

"Sure," put in Blake. "We've had enough liquid refreshments to do any one. If I don't look out, you'll both be drinking river water. Just bear in mind the work I'd have to carve a pair of gravestones. No; that flask has got to do you till we get home. I don't shin up any more telegraph poles to-day."

"Would it not be best for Mr. Winthrope to rest during the noon hours?"

"'Fraid not, Miss Jenny. We're not on t'other side of Jordan yet, and there's no rest for the weary this side."

"What odd expressions you use, Mr. Blake!"

"Just giving you the reverse application of one of those songs they jolly us with in the mission churches—"

"I'm sure, Mr. Blake—"

"Me, too, Miss Jenny! So, as that's settled, we'll be moving. Chuck some live coals in the pot, and come on."

He started off, weapons in hand. Winthrope made a languid effort to take possession of the pot. But Miss Leslie pushed him aside, and wrapping all in the antelope skin, slung it upon her back.

"The brute!" exclaimed Winthrope. "To leave such a load for you, when he knew that I can do so little!"

The girl met his outburst with a brave attempt at a smile. "Please try to look at the bright side, Mr. Winthrope. Really, I believe he thinks it is best for us to exert ourselves."

"He has other opinions with which we of the cultured class would hardly agree, Miss Leslie. Consider his command that we shall go thirsty until he permits us to return to the cliffs. The man's impertinence is intolerable. I shall go to the river and drink when I choose."

"Oh, but the danger of malaria!"

"Nonsense. Malaria, like yellow fever, comes only from the bite of certain species of mosquitoes. If we have the fever, it will be entirely his fault. We have been bitten repeatedly this morning, and all because he must compel us to come with him to this infected lowland."

"Still, I think we should do what Mr. Blake says."

"My dear Miss Genevieve, for your sake I will endeavor not to break with the fellow. Only, you know, it is deuced hard to keep one's temper when one considers what a bounder—what an unmitigated cad—"

"Stop! I will not listen to another word!" exclaimed the girl, and she hurried after Blake, leaving Winthrope staring in astonishment.

"My word!" he muttered; "can it be, after all I've done—and him, of all the low fellows—"

He stood for several moments in deep thought. The look on his sallow face was far from pleasant.

CHAPTER XVII

THE SERPENT STRIKES

When Winthrope came up with the others, they were gathering green leaves to throw on the fire which was blazing close beside the ant-hill.

"Get a move on you!" called Blake. "You're slow. Grab a bunch of leaves, and get into the smoke, if you don't want to be stung."

Winthrope neither gathered any leaves nor hurried himself, until he was visited by a highly irritated bee. Then he obeyed with alacrity. Blake was far too intent on other matters to heed the Englishman. Leaping in and out of the thick of the smoke, he pounded the ant-hill with his club, until he had broken a gaping hole into the cavity. The smoke, pouring into the hive, made short work of the bees that had not already been suffocated.

Although the antelope skin was drawn into the shape of a sack, both it and the pot were filled to overflowing with honey, and there were still more combs left than the three could eat.

Blake caught Winthrope smiling with satisfaction as he licked his fingers.

"What's the matter with my expedition now, old man?" he demanded.

"I—ah—must admit, Blake, we have had a most enjoyable change of food."

"If you are sure it will agree with you," remarked Miss Leslie.

"But I am sure of that, Miss Genevieve. I could digest anything to-day. I'm fairly ravenous."

"All the more reason to be careful," rejoined Blake. "I guess, though, what we've had'll do no harm. We'll let it settle a bit, here in the shade, and then hit the home trail."

"Could we not first go to the river, Mr. Blake? My hands are dreadfully sticky."

"Win will take you. It's only a little way to the bank here and there's not much underbrush."

"If you think it's quite safe—" remarked Winthrope.

"It's safe enough. Go on. You'll see the river in half a minute. Only thing, you'd better watch out for alligators."

"I believe that—er—properly speaking, these are crocodiles."

"You don't say! Heap of difference it will make if one gets you."

Miss Leslie caught Winthrope's eye. He turned on his heel, and led the way for her through the first thicket. Beyond this they came to a little glade which ran through to the river. When they reached the bank, they stepped cautiously down the muddy slope, and bathed their hands in the clear water. As Miss Leslie rose, Winthrope bent over and began to drink.

"Oh, Mr. Winthrope!" she exclaimed; "please don't! In your weak condition, I'm so afraid—"

"Do not alarm yourself. I am perfectly well, and I am quite as competent to judge what is good for me as your—ah—countryman."

"Mr. Winthrope, I am thinking only of your own good."

Winthrope took another deep draught, rinsed his fingers fastidiously, and arose.

"My dear Miss Genevieve," he observed, "a woman looks at these matters in such a different light from a man. But you should know that there are some things a gentleman cannot tolerate."

"You were welcome to all the water in the flask. Surely with that you could have waited, if only to please me."

"Ah, if you put it that way, I must beg pardon. Anything to please you, I'm sure! Pray forgive me, and forget the incident. It is now past."

"I hope so!" she murmured; but her heart sank as she glanced at his sallow face, and she recalled his languid, feeble movements.

Piqued by her look, Winthrope started back through the glade. Miss Leslie was turning to follow, when she caught sight of a gorgeous crimson blossom under the nearest tree. It was the first flower she had seen since being shipwrecked. She uttered a little cry of delight, and ran to pluck the blossom.

Winthrope, glancing about at her exclamation, saw her stoop over the flower—and in the same instant he saw a huge vivid coil, all black and green and yellow, flash up out of the bedded leaves and strike against the girl. She staggered back, screaming with horror, yet seemed unable to run.

Winthrope swung up his stick, and dashed across the glade towards her.

"What is it—a snake?" he cried.

The girl did not seem to hear him. She had ceased screaming, and stood rigid with fright, glaring down at the ground before her. In a moment Winthrope was near enough, to make out the brilliant glistening body, now extended full length in the grass. It was nearly five feet long and thick as his thigh. Another step, and he saw the hideous triangular head, lifted a few inches on the thick neck. The cold eyes were fixed upon the girl in a malignant, deadly stare.

"Snake! snake!" he yelled, and thrust his cane at the reptile's tail.

Again came a flashing leap of the beautiful ornate coil, and the stick was struck from Winthrope's hand. He danced backward, wild with excitement.

"Snake!–Hi, Blake! monster!–Run, Miss Leslie! I'll hold him–I'll get another stick!"

He darted aside to catch up a branch, and then ran in and struck boldly at the adder, which reared hissing to meet him. But the blow fell short, and the rotten wood shattered on the ground. Again Winthrope ran aside for a stick. There was none near, and as he paused to glance about, Blake came sprinting down the glade.

"Where?" he shouted.

"There–Hi! look out! You'll be on him!"

Blake stopped short, barely beyond striking distance of the hissing reptile.

"Wow!" he yelled. "Puff adder! I'll fix him."

He leaped back, and thrust his bow at the snake. The challenge was met by a vicious lunge. Even where he stood Winthrope heard the thud of the reptile's head upon the ground.

"Now, once more, tootsie!" mocked Blake, swinging up his club.

Again the adder struck at the bow tip, more viciously than before. With the flash of the stroke, Blake's right foot thrust forward, and his club came down with all the drive of his sinewy arm behind it. The blow fell across the thickest part of the adder's outstretched body.

"Told you so! See him wiggle!" shouted Blake. "Broke his back, first lick– What's the matter, Miss Jenny? He can't do anything now."

Miss Leslie did not answer. She stood rigid, her face ashy-gray, her dilated eyes fixed upon the writhing, hissing adder.

"I–I think the snake struck her!" gasped Winthrope, suddenly overcome with horror.

"God!" cried Blake. He dropped his club, and rushed to the girl. In a moment he had knelt before her and flung up her leopard-skin skirt. Her stockings ripped to shreds in his frantic grasp. There, a little below her right knee, was a tiny red wound. Blake put his lips to it, and sucked with fierce energy.

Then the girl found her voice.

"Go away–go away! How dare you!" she cried, as her face flushed scarlet.

117

Blake turned, spat, and burst out with a loud demand of Winthrope: "Quick! the little knife—I'll have to slash it! Ten times worse than a rattlesnake— Lord! you're slow—I'll use mine!"

"Let go of me—let go! What do you mean, sir?" cried the girl, struggling to free herself.

"Hold still, you little fool!" he shouted. "It's death—sure death, if I don't get the poison from that bite!"

"I'm not bitten— Let go, I say! It struck in the fold of my skirt."

"For God's sake, Jenny, don't lie! It's certain death! I saw the mark—"

"That was a thorn. I drew it out an hour ago."

Blake looked up into her hazel eyes. They were blazing with indignant scorn. He freed her, and rose with clumsy slowness. Again he glanced at her quivering, scarlet face, only to look away with a sheepish expression.

"I guess you think I'm just a damned meddlesome idiot," he mumbled.

She did not answer. He stood for a little, rubbing a finger across his sun-blistered lips. Suddenly he stopped and looked at the finger. It was streaked with blood.

"Whew!" he exclaimed. "Didn't stop to think of that! It's just as well for me, Miss Jenny, that wasn't an adder bite. A little poison on my sore lip would have done for me. Ten to one, we'd both have turned up our toes at the same time. Of course, though, that'd be nothing to you."

Miss Leslie put her hands before her face, and burst into hysterical weeping.

Blake looked around, far more alarmed than when facing the adder.

"Here, you blooming lud!" he shouted; "take the lady away, and be quick about it. She'll go dotty if she sees any more snake stunts. Clear out with her, while I smash the wriggler."

Winthrope, who had been staring fixedly at the beautiful coloring and loathsome form of the writhing adder, started at Blake's harsh command as though struck.

"I—er—to be sure," he stammered, and darting around to the hysterical girl, he took her arm and hurried her away up the glade.

They had gone several paces when Blake came running up behind them. Winthrope looked back with a glance of inquiry. Blake shook his head.

"Not yet," he said. "Give me your cigarette case. I've thought of something– Hold on; take out the cigarettes. Smoke 'em, if you like."

Case in hand, Blake returned to the wounded adder, and picked up his club. A second smashing blow would have ended the matter at once; but Blake did not strike. Instead, he feinted with his club until he managed to pin down the venomous head. The club lay across the monster's neck, and he held it fast with the pressure of his foot.

When, half an hour later, he wiped his knife on a wisp of grass and stood up, the cigarette case contained over a tablespoonful of a crystalline liquid. He peered in at it, his heavy jaw thrust out, his eyes glowing with savage elation.

"Talk about your meat trusts and Winchesters!" he exulted; "here's a whole carload of beef in this little box—enough dope to morgue a herd of steers. Good God, though, that was a close shave for her!"

His face sobered, and he stood for several moments staring thoughtfully into space. Then his gaze chanced to fall upon the great crimson blossom which had so nearly lured the girl to her death.

"Hello!" he exclaimed; "that's an amaryllis. Wonder if she wasn't coming to pick it–" He snapped shut the lid of the cigarette case, thrust it carefully into his shirt pocket, and stepped forward to pluck the flower. "Makes a fellow feel like a kid; but maybe it'll make her feel less sore at me."

He stood gazing at the flower for several moments, his eyes aglow with a soft blue light.

"Whew!" he sighed; "if only– But what's the use? She's 'way out of my class—a rough brute like me! All the same, it's up to me to take care of her. She can't keep me from being her friend—and she sure can't object to my picking flowers for her."

Amaryllis in hand, he gathered up his bow and club. Then he paused to study the skin of the decapitated adder. The inspection ended with a shake of his head.

"Better not, Thomas. It would make a dandy quiver; but then, it might get on her nerves."

When he came to the ant-hill, he found companions and honey alike gone. He went on to the cocoanuts. There he came upon Winthrope stretched flat beside the skin of honey. Miss Leslie was seated a little way beyond, nervously bending a palm-leaf into shape for a hat.

"I say, Blake," drawled Winthrope, "you've been a deuced long time in coming. It was no end of a task to lug the honey—"

Blake brushed past without replying, and went on until he stood before the girl. As she glanced up at him, he held out the crimson blossom.

"Thought you might like posies," he said, in a hesitating voice.

Instead of taking the flower, she drew back with a gesture of repulsion.

"Oh, take it away!" she exclaimed.

Blake flung the rejected gift on the ground, and crushed it beneath his heel.

"Catch me making a fool of myself again!" he growled.

"I—I did not mean it that way—really I didn't, Mr. Blake. It was the thought of that awful snake."

But Blake, cut to the quick, had turned away, far too angry to heed what she said. He stopped short beside the Englishman; but only to sling the skin of honey upon his back. The load was by no means a light one, even for his strength. Yet he caught up the heavy pot as well, and made off across the plain at a pace which the others could not hope to equal.

As Winthrope rose and came forward to join Miss Leslie, he looked about closely for the bruised flower. It was nowhere in sight.

"Er—beg pardon, Miss Genevieve, but did not Blake drop the bloom—er—blossom somewhere about here?"

"Perhaps he did," replied Miss Leslie. She spoke with studied indifference.

"I—ah—saw the fellow exhibit his impudence."

"Ye-es?"

"You know, I think it high time the bounder is taken down a peg."

"Ah, indeed! Then why do you not try it?"

"Miss Genevieve! you know that at present I am physically so much his inferior—"

"How about mentally?"

Though the girl's eyes were veiled by their lashes, she saw Winthrope cast after Blake a look that seemed to her almost fiercely vindictive.

"Well?" she said, smiling, but watching him closely.

"Mentally!—We'll soon see about that!" he muttered. "I must say, Miss Genevieve, it strikes me as deuced odd, you know, to hear you speak so pleasantly of a person who—not to mention past occurrences—has to-day, with the most shocking disregard of—er—decency—"

"Stop!—stop this instant!" screamed the girl, her nerves overwrought.

Winthrope smiled with complacent assurance.

"My dear young lady," he drawled, "allow me to repeat, 'All is fair in love and war.' Believe me, I love you most ardently."

"No gentleman would press his suit at such a time as this!"

"Really now, I fancy I have always comported myself as a gentleman—"

"A trifle too much so, truth to say!" she retorted.

"Ah, indeed. However, this is now quite another matter. Has it not occurred to you, my dear, that this entire experience of ours since that beastly storm is rather—er—compromising?"

"You—you dare say such a thing! I'll go this instant and tell Mr. Blake! I'll—"

"Begging your pardon, madam,—but are you prepared to marry that barbarous clodhopper?"

"Marry? What do you mean, sir?"

"Precisely that. It is a question of marriage, if you'll pardon me. And, you see, I flatter myself, that when it comes to the point, it will not be Blake, but myself—"

"Ah, indeed! And if I should prefer neither of you?"

"Begging your pardon,—I fancy you will honor me with your hand, my dear. For one thing, you admit that I am a gentleman."

"Oh, indeed!"

"One moment, please! I am trying to intimate to you, as delicately as possible, how—er—embarrassing you would find it to have these little occurrences—above all, to-day's—noised abroad to the vulgar crowd, or even among your friends—"

"What do you mean? What do you want?" cried the girl, staring at him with a deepening fear in her bewildered eyes.

"Believe me, my dear, it grieves me to so perturb you; but—er—love must have its way, you know."

"You forget. There is Mr. Blake."

"Ah, to be sure! But really now, you would not ask, or even permit him to murder me; and one is not legally bound, you know, to observe promises—a pledge of silence, for example—when extorted under duress, under violence, you know."

Miss Leslie looked the Englishman up and down, her brown eyes sparkling with quick-returning anger. He met her scorn with a smile of smug complacency.

"Cad!" she cried, and turning her back upon him, she set out across the plain after Blake.

CHAPTER XVIII

THE EAVESDROPPER CAUGHT

Even had it not been for her doubts of Blake, the girl's modesty would have caused her to think twice before repeating to him the Englishman's insulting proposal. While she yet hesitated and delayed, Winthrope came down with a second attack of fever. Blake, who until then had held himself sullenly apart from him as well as from Miss Leslie, at once softened to a gentler, or, at least, to a more considerate mood. Though his speech and bearing continued morose, he took upon himself all the duties of night nurse, besides working and foraging several hours each day.

Much to Miss Leslie's surprise, she found herself tending the invalid through the daytime almost as though nothing had happened. But everything about this wild and perilous life was so strange and unnatural to her that she found herself accepting the most unconventional relations as a regular consequence of the situation. She was feverishly eager for anything that might occupy her mind; for she felt that to brood over the future might mean madness. The mere thought of the possibilities was far too terrifying to be calmly dwelt upon. Though slight, there had been some little comfort in the belief that she could rely on Winthrope. But now she was left alone with her doubt and dread. Even if she had nothing to fear from Blake, there were all the savage dangers of the coast, and behind those, far worse, the fever.

Meantime Blake went about his share of the camp work, gruff and silent, but with the usual concrete results. He brought load after load of fresh cocoanuts, and took great pains to hunt out the deliciously flavored eggs of the frigate birds to tempt Winthrope's failing appetite. When Miss Leslie suggested that beef juice would be much better for the invalid than broth, he went out immediately in search of a gum-bearing tree, and that night, after heating a small quantity of gum in the cigarette case with the adder poison, he spent hours replacing his arrow-heads with small barbed tips that could be loosened from their sockets by a slight pull.

A little before dawn he dipped two of his new arrow-heads in the sticky contents of the cigarette case, fitted them carefully to their shafts, and stole away down the cleft. Dawn found him crouched low in the grass where the overflow from the pool ran out into the plain along its little channel. He could see large forms moving away from him; then came the flood of crimson light, and he made out that the figures were a drove of huge eland.

His eyes flashed with eagerness. It was a long shot; but he knew that no more was required than to pierce the skin on any part of his quarry's body. He put his fingers between his teeth, and sent out a piercing whistle. It was a trick he had tried more than once on deer and pronghorn antelope. As he expected, the eland halted and swung half around. Their ox-like sides presented a mark hard to miss.

He rose and shot as they were wheeling to fly. Before he could fit his second arrow to the string, the whole herd were running off at a lumbering gallop. He lowered his bow, and walked after the animals, smiling with grim anticipation. He had seen his arrow strike against the side of the young bull at which he had aimed.

A little beyond where the bull had stood, he came upon the headless shaft of his arrow. As he stooped and caught it up, he saw one of the fleeing animals fall. When he came up with the dead bull, his first act was to recover his arrow-tip and cut out the flesh around the wound. Provided only with his weak-bladed knife, he found it no easy task to butcher so large a beast. Though he had now acquired considerable dexterity in the art, noon had passed before he brought the first load of meat up the cleft.

So great was the abundance of meat that Blake worked all the remainder of the day and all night stringing the flesh on the curing racks, and Miss Leslie tried out pot after pot of fat and tallow, until every spare vessel was filled, and she had to resort to a hollow in the rock beside the spring. Blake promised to make more pots as soon as he could fetch the clay, but he had first to dress the eland hide, and prepare a new stock of thread and cord from parts of the animal which he was careful not to let her see.

Whatever their concern for the future,—and even Blake's was keen and bitter,—the party, as a party, for the time being might have been considered extremely fortunate. They had a shelter secure alike from the weather and from wild beasts; an abundance of nutritious food, and, as material for clothing, the bushbuck, hyena, and eland hides. To obtain more skins and more meat Blake now knew would be a simple matter so long as he had enough poison left in the cigarette case to moisten the tips of his arrows.

Even Winthrope's relapse proved far less serious than might reasonably have been expected. The fever soon left him, and within a few days he regained strength enough to care for himself. Here, however, much to Blake's perplexity and concern, his progress seemed to stop, and all Blake's urging could do no more than cause him to move languidly from one shady spot to another. He would receive Blake's orders with a smile and a drawling "Ya-as, to be sure!"—and would then absolutely ignore the matter.

Only in two ways did the invalid exhibit any signs of energy. He could and did eat with a heartiness little short of that shown by Blake, and he would insist upon seeking opportunities to press his attentions upon Miss Leslie. He was careful to avoid all offensive remarks; yet the veriest commonplace from his lips was now an offence to the girl. While he needed her as nurse, she had endured his talk as part of her duty. But now she felt that she could no longer do so. Taking advantage of a time when the Englishman was, as she supposed, enjoying a noonday siesta down towards the barricade, she went to meet Blake, who had been up on the cliff for eggs.

"Hello!" he sang out, as he swung down the tree, one hand gripping the clay pot in which he had gathered the eggs. "What you doing out in the sun? Get into the shade."

She stepped into the shade, and waited until he had climbed down the pile of stones which he had built for steps at the foot of the tree.

"Mr. Blake," she began, "could not I do this work,—gather the eggs?"

"You could, if I'd let you, Miss Jenny. But it strikes me you've got quite enough to do. Tell you the truth, I'd like to make Win take it in hand again. But all my cussing won't budge him an inch, and you know, when it comes to the rub, I couldn't wallop a fellow who can hardly stand up."

"Is he really so weak?" she murmured.

"Well, you know how— Say, you don't mean that you think he's shamming?"

"I did not say that I thought so, Mr. Blake. I do not care to talk about him. What I wish is that you will let me attend to this work."

"Couldn't think of it, Miss Jenny! You're already doing your share."

"Mr. Blake,—if you must know,—I wish to have a place where I can go and be apart—alone."

Blake scowled. "Alone with that dude! He'd soon find enough strength to climb up with you on the cliff."

"I—ah—Mr. Blake, would he be apt to follow me, if I told you distinctly I should rather be alone?"

"Would he? Well, I should rather guess not!" cried Blake, making no attempt to conceal his delight. "I'll give him a hint that'll make his hair curl. From now on, nobody climbs up this tree but you, without first asking your permission."

"Thank you, Mr. Blake! You are very kind."

"Kind to let you do more work! But say, I'll help out all I can on the other work. You know, Miss Jenny,—a rough fellow like me don't know how to say it, but he can think it just the same,—I'd do anything in the world for you!"

As he spoke, he held out his rough, powerful hand. She shrank back a little, and caught her breath in sudden fright. But when she met his steady gaze, her fear left her as quickly as it had come. She impulsively thrust out her hand, and he seized it in a grip that brought the tears to her eyes.

"Miss Jenny! Miss Jenny!" he murmured, utterly unconscious that he was hurting her, "you know now that I'm your friend, Miss Jenny!"

"Yes, Mr. Blake," she answered, blushing and drawing her hand free. "I believe you are a friend—I believe I can trust you."

"You can, by—Jiminy! But say," he continued, blundering with dense stupidity, "do you really mean that? Can you forgive me for being so confounded meddlesome, the other day, after the snake—"

He stopped short, for upon the instant she was facing him, as on that eventful day, scarlet with shame and anger.

"How dare you speak of it?" she cried. "You're—you're not a gentleman!"

Before he could reply, she turned and left him, walking rapidly and with her head held high. Blake stared after her in bewilderment.

"Well, what in—what in thunder have I done now?" he exclaimed. "Ladies are certainly mighty funny! To go off at a touch—and just when I thought we were going to be chums! But then, of course, I've the whole thing to learn about nice girls—like her!"

"I—ah—must certainly agree with you there, Blake," drawled Winthrope, from beside the nearest bush.

Blake turned upon him with savage fury: "You dirty sneak!—you *gentleman!* You've been eavesdropping!"

The Englishman's yellow face paled to a sallow mottled gray. He had seen the same look in Blake's eyes twice before, and this time Blake was far more angry.

"You sneak!—you sham gent!" repeated the American, his voice sinking ominously.

Winthrope dropped in an abject heap, as though Blake had struck him with his club.

"No, no!" he protested shrilly. "I am a real—I am—I'm a not—"

"That's it—you're a not! That's true!" broke in Blake, with sudden grim humor. "You're a nothing. A fellow can't even wipe his shoes on nothing!"

The change to sarcasm came as an immense relief to Winthrope.

"Ah, I say now, Blake," he drawled, pulling together his assurance the instant the dangerous light left Blake's eyes, "I say now, do you think it fair to pick on a man who is so much your—er—who is ill and weak?"

"That's it—do the baby act," jeered Blake. "But say, I don't know just how much eavesdropping you did; so there's one thing I'll repeat for the special benefit of your ludship. It'll be good for your delicate health to pay attention. From now on, the cliff top belongs to Miss Leslie. Gents and book agents not allowed. Understand? You don't go up there without her special invite. If you do, I'll twist your damned neck!"

He turned on his heel, and left the Englishman cowering.

CHAPTER XIX

AN OMINOUS LULL

The three saw nothing more of each other that day. Miss Leslie had withdrawn into the baobab, and Blake had gone off down the cleft for more salt. He did not return until after the others were asleep. Miss Leslie had gone without her supper, or had eaten some of the food stored within the tree.

When, late the next morning, she finally left her seclusion, Blake was nowhere in sight. Ignoring Winthrope's attempts to start a conversation, she hurried through her breakfast, and having gathered a supply of food and water, went to spend the day on the headland.

Evening forced her to return to the cleft. She had emptied the water flask by noon, and was thirsty. Winthrope was dozing beneath his canopy, which Blake had moved some yards down towards the barricade. Blake was cooking supper.

He did not look up, and met her attempt at a pleasant greeting with an inarticulate grunt. When she turned to enter the baobab, she found the opening littered with bamboos and green creepers and pieces of large branches with charred ends. On either side, midway through the entrance, a vertical row of holes had been sunk through the bark of the tree into the soft wood.

"What is this?" she asked. "Are you planning a porch?"

"Maybe," he replied.

"But why should you make the holes so far in? I know so little about these matters, but I should have fancied the holes would come on the front of the tree."

"You'll see in a day or two."

"How did you make the holes? They look black, as though—"

"Burnt 'em, of course—hot stones."

"That was so clever of you!"

He made no response.

Supper was eaten in silence. Even Winthrope's presence would have been a relief to the girl; yet she could not go to waken him, or even suggest that her companion do so. Blake sat throughout the meal sullen and stolid, and carefully avoided meeting her gaze. Before they had finished, twilight had come and gone, and night was upon them. Yet she lingered for a last attempt.

"Good-night, friend!" she whispered.

He sprang up as though she had struck him, and blundered away into the darkness.

In the morning it was as before. He had gone off before she wakened. She lingered over breakfast; but he did not appear, and she could not endure Winthrope's suave drawl. She went for another day on the headland.

She returned somewhat earlier than on the previous day. As before, Winthrope was dozing in the shade. But Blake was under the baobab, raking together a heap of rubbish. His hands were scratched and bleeding. To the girl's surprise, he met her with a cheerful grin and a clear, direct glance.

"Look here," he called.

She stepped around the baobab, and stood staring. The entrance, from the ground to the height of twelve feet, was walled up with a mass of thorny branches, interwoven with yet thornier creepers.

"How's that for a front door?" he demanded.

"Door?"

"Yes."

"But it's so big. I could never move it."

"A child could. Look." He grasped a projecting handle near the bottom of the thorny mass. The lower half of the door swung up and outward, the upper half in and downward. "See; it's balanced on a crossbar in the middle. Come on in."

She walked after him in under the now horizontal door. He gave the inner end a light upward thrust, and the door swung back in its vertical circle until it again stood upright in the opening. From the inside the girl could see the strong framework to which was lashed the facing of thorns. It was made of bamboo and strong pieces of branches, bound together with tough creepers.

"Pretty good grating, eh?" remarked Blake. "When those green creepers dry, they'll shrink and hold tight as iron clamps. Even now nothing short of a rhinoceros could walk through when the bars are fast. See here."

He stepped up to the novel door, and slid several socketed crossbars until their outer ends were deep in the holes in the tree trunk, three on each side.

"How's that for a set of bolts?" he demanded.

"Wonderful! Really, you are very, very clever! But why should you go to all this trouble, when the barricade—"

"Well, you see, it's best to be on the safe side."

"But it's absurd for you to go to all this needless work. Not that I do not appreciate your kind thought for my safety. Yet look at your hands!"

Blake hastened to put his bleeding hands behind him.

"They are no sight for a lady!" he muttered apologetically.

"Go and wash them at once, and I'll put on a dressing."

Blake glowed with frank pleasure, yet shook his head.

"No, thank you, Miss Jenny. You needn't bother. They'll do all right."

"You must! It would please me."

"Why, then, of course— But first, I want to make sure you understand fastening the door. Try the bars yourself."

She obeyed, sliding the bars in and out until he nodded his satisfaction.

"Good!" he said. "Now promise me you'll slide 'em fast every night."

"If you ask it. But why?"

"I want to make perfectly safe."

"Safe? But am I not secure with—"

"Look here, Miss Leslie; I'm not going to say anything about anybody."

"Perhaps you had better say no more, Mr. Blake."

"That's right. But whatever happens, you'll believe I've done my best, won't you?—even if I'm not a— Promise me straight, you'll lock up tight every night."

"Very well, I promise," responded the girl, not a little troubled by the strangeness of his expression.

He turned at once, swung open the door, and went out. During supper he was markedly taciturn, and immediately afterwards went off to his bed.

That night Miss Leslie dutifully fastened herself in with all six bars. She wakened at dawn, and hastened out to prepare Blake's breakfast, but she found herself too late. There were evidences that he had eaten and gone off before dawn. The stretching frame of one of the antelope skins had been moved around by the fire, and on the smooth inner surface of the hide was a laconic note, written with charcoal in a firm, bold hand:—

"*Exploring inland. Back by night, if can.*"

She bit her lip in her disappointment, for she had planned to show him how much she appreciated his absurd but well-meant concern for her safety. As it was, he had gone off without a word, and left her to the questionable pleasure of a *tête-à-tête* with Winthrope. Hoping to avoid this, she hurried her preparations for a day on the cliff. But before she could get off, Winthrope sauntered up, hiding his yawns behind a hand which had regained most of its normal plumpness. His eye was at once caught by the charcoal note.

"Ah!" he drawled; "really now, this is too kind of him to give us the pleasure of his absence all day!"

"Ye-es!" murmured Miss Leslie. "Permit me to add that you will also have the pleasure of my absence. I am going now."

Winthrope looked down, and began to speak very rapidly: "Miss Genevieve, I–I wish to apologize. I've thought it over. I've made a mistake–I–I mean, my conduct the other day was vile, utterly vile! Permit me to appeal to your considerateness for a man who has been unfortunate–who, I mean, has been–er–was carried away by his feelings. Your favoring of that bloom–er–that–er–bounder so angered me that I–that I–"

"Mr. Winthrope!" interrupted the girl, "I will have you to understand that you do not advance yourself in my esteem by such references to Mr. Blake."

"Aye! aye, that Blake!" panted Winthrope. "Don't you see? It's 'im, an' that blossom! W'en a man's daffy–w'en 'e's in love!–"

Miss Leslie burst into a nervous laugh; but checked herself on the instant.

"Really, Mr. Winthrope!" she exclaimed, "you must pardon me. I–I never knew that cultured Englishmen ever dropped their h's. As it happens, you know, I never saw one excited before this."

"Ah, yes; to be sure–to be sure!" murmured Winthrope, in an odd tone.

The girl threw out her hand in a little gesture of protest.

"Really, I'm sorry to have hurt–to have been so thoughtless!"

Winthrope stood silent. She spoke again: "I'll do what you ask. I'll make allowances for your–for your feelings towards me, and will try to forget all you said the other day. Let me begin by asking a favor of you."

"Ah, Miss Genevieve, anything, to be sure, that I may do!"

"It is that I wish your opinion. When Mr. Blake finished that absurd door last evening, he would not tell me why he had built it–only a vague statement about my safety."

"Ah! He did not go into particulars?" drawled Winthrope.

"No, not even a hint; and he looked so—odd."

Winthrope slowly rubbed his soft palms on upon the other.

"Do you—er—really desire to know his—the motive which actuated him?" he murmured.

"I should not have mentioned it to you, if I did not," she answered.

"Well—er—" He hesitated and paused for a full minute. "You see, it is a rather difficult undertaking to intimate such a matter to a lady—just the right touch of delicacy, you know. But I will begin by explaining that I have known it since the first—"

"Known what?"

"Of that bound—of—er—Blake's trouble."

"Trouble?"

"Ah! Perhaps I should have said affliction; yes, that is the better word. To own the truth, the fellow has some good qualities. It was no doubt because he realised, when in his better moments—"

"Better moments? Mr. Winthrope, I am not a child. In justice both to myself and to Mr. Blake, I must ask you to speak out plainly."

"My dear Miss Leslie, may I first ask if you have not observed how strangely at times the fellow acts,—'looks odd,' as you put it,—how he falls into melancholia or senseless rages? I may truthfully state that he has three times threatened my life."

"I—I thought his anger quite natural, after I had so rudely—and so many people are given to brooding— But if he was violent to you—"

"My dear Miss Genevieve, I hold nothing against the miserable fellow. At such times he is not—er—responsible, you know. Let us give the fellow full credit—that is why he himself built your door."

"Oh, but I can't believe it! I can't believe it!" cried the girl. "It's not possible! He's so strong, so true and manly, so kind, for all his gruffness!"

"Ah, my dear!" soothed Winthrope, "that is the pity of it. But when a man must needs be his worst enemy, when he must needs lead a certain kind of life, he must take the consequences. To put it as delicately as possible, yet explain all, I need only say one word—paranoia."

Miss Leslie gathered up her day's outfit with trembling fingers, and went to mount the cliff.

After waiting a few minutes Winthrope walked hurriedly through the cleft, and climbed the tree-ladder with an agility that would have amazed his companions. But he did not draw himself up on the cliff.

Having satisfied himself that Miss Leslie was well out toward the signal, he returned to the baobab, and proceeded to examine Blake's door with minute scrutiny.

That evening, shortly before dark, Blake came in almost exhausted by his journey. Few men could have covered the same ground in twice the time. It had been one continuous round of grass jungle, thorn scrub, rocks, and swamp. And for all his pains, he brought back with him nothing more than the discouraging information that the back-country was worse than the shore. Yet he betrayed no trace of depression over the bad news, and for all his fatigue, maintained a tone of hearty cheerfulness until, having eaten his fill, he suddenly observed Miss Leslie's frigid politeness.

"What's up now?" he demanded. "You're not mad 'cause I hiked off this morning without notice?"

"No, of course not, Mr. Blake. Nothing of the kind. But I—"

"Well,-what?" he broke in, as she hesitated. "I can't, for the world, think of anything else I've done—"

"You've done! Perhaps I might suggest that it is a question of what you haven't done." The girl was trembling on the verge of hysterics. "Yes, what you've not done! All these weeks, and not a single attempt to get us away from here, except that miserable signal; and I as good as put that up! You call yourself a man! But I–I–" She stopped short, white with a sudden overpowering fear.

Winthrope looked from her to Blake with a sidelong glance, his lips drawn up in an odd twist.

There followed several moments of tense silence; then Blake mumbled apologetically: "Well, I suppose I might have done more. I was so dead anxious to make sure of food and shelter. But this trip to-day—"

"Mr.–Mr. Blake, pray do not get excited–I–I mean, please excuse me. I'm—"

"You're coming down sick!" he said.

"No, no! I have no fever."

"Then it's the sun. Yet you ought to keep up there where the air is freshest. I'll make you a shade."

She protested, and withdrew, somewhat hurriedly, to her tree.

In the morning Blake was gone again; but instead of a note, beside the fire stood the smaller antelope skin, converted into a great bamboo-ribbed sunshade.

She spent the day as usual on the headland. There was no wind, and the sun was scorching hot. But with her big sunshade to protect her from the direct rays, the heat was at least endurable. She even found energy to work at a basket which she was attempting to weave out of long, coarse grass; yet there were frequent intervals when her hands sank idle in her lap, and she gazed away over the shimmering glassy expanse of the ocean.

In the afternoon the heat became oppressively sultry, and a long slow swell began to roll shoreward from beyond the distant horizon, showing no trace of white along its oily crests until they broke over the coral reefs. There was not a breath of air stirring, and for a time the reefs so checked the rollers that they lacked force to drive on in and break upon the beach.

Steadily, however, the swell grew heavier, though not so much as a cat's-paw ruffled the dead surfaces of the watery hillocks. By sunset they were rolling high over both lines of reefs and racing shoreward to break upon the beach and the cliff foot in furious surf. The still air reverberated with the booming of the breakers. Yet the girl, inland bred and unversed in weather lore, sat heedless and indifferent, her eyes fixed upon the horizon in a vacant stare.

Her reverie was at last disturbed by the peculiar behavior of the seafowl. Those in the air circled around in a manner strange to her, while their mates on the ledges waddled restlessly about over and between their nests. There was a shriller note than usual in their discordant clamor.

Yet even when she gave heed to the birds, the girl failed to realize their alarm or to sense the impending danger. It was only that a feeling of disquiet had broken the spell of her reverie; it did not obtrude upon the field of her conscious thought. She sighed, and rose to return to the cleft, idly wondering that the air should seem more sultry than at mid-day. The peculiar appearance of the sun and the western sky meant nothing more to her than an odd effect of color and light. She smilingly compared it with an attempt at a sunset painted by an artist friend of the impressionist school.

Neither Winthrope nor Blake was in sight when she reached the baobab, and neither appeared, though she delayed supper until dark. It was quite possible that they had eaten before her return and had gone off again, the Englishman to doze, and Blake on an evening hunt.

At last, tired of waiting, she covered the fire, and retired into her tree-cave. The air in the cleft was still more stifling than on the headland. She paused, with her hand upraised to close the swinging door. She had propped it open when she came out in the morning. After a moment's hesitation, she went on across the hollow, leaving the door wide open.

"I will rest a little, and close it later," she sighed. She was feeling weary and depressed.

An hour passed. An ominous stillness lay upon the cleft. Even the cicadas had hushed their shrill note. The only sound was a muffled reverberating echo of the surf roaring upon the seashore. Beneath the giant spread of the baobab all was blackness.

Something moved in a bush a little way down the cleft. A crouching figure appeared, dimly outlined in the starlight. The figure crept stealthily across into the denser night of the baobab. The darkness closed about it like a shroud.

A blinding flash of light pierced the blackness. The figure halted and crouched lower, though the flash had gone again in a fraction of a second. A dull rumbling mingled with the ceaseless boom of the surf.

A second flash lighted the cleft with its dazzling coruscation. This time the creeping figure did not halt.

Again and again the forked lightning streaked across the sky, every stroke more vivid than the one before. The rumble of the distant thunder deepened to a heavy rolling which dominated the dull roar of the breakers. The storm was coming with the on-rush of a tornado. Yet the leaves hung motionless in the still air, and there was no sound other than the thunder and the booming of the surf.

The lightning flared, one stroke upon the other, with a brilliancy that lit up the cave's interior brighter than at mid-day.

In the white glare the girl saw Winthrope, crouched beneath her upswung door; and his face was as the face of a beast.

CHAPTER XX

THE HURRICANE BLAST

For a moment that seemed a moment of eternity, she lay on her bed, staring into the blank darkness. The storm burst with a crashing uproar that brought her to her feet, with a shriek. Her giant tree creaked and strained under the impact of the terrific hurricane blasts that came howling through the cleft like a rout of shrieking fiends. The peals of thunder merged into one continuous roar, beneath which the solid ledges of rock jarred and quivered. The sky was a pall of black clouds, meshed with a dazzling network of forked lightning.

The girl stood motionless, stunned by the uproar, appalled by the blinding glare of the thunder-bolts; yet even more fearful of the figure which every flash showed her still lurking beneath the door. A gust-borne bough struck with numbing force against her upraised arm. But she took no heed. She was unaware of the swirl of rain and sticks and leaves that was driving in through the open entrance.

On a sudden the door shook free from its props and whirled violently around on its balance-bar. There was a shriek that pierced above the shrilling of the cyclone,–a single human shriek.

The girl sprang across the cave. The heavy door swished up before her and down again, its lower edge all but grazing her face. For a moment it stopped in a vertical position, and hung quivering, like a beast about to leap upon its prey. Too excited to comprehend the danger of the act, the girl sprang forward and shot one of the thick bars into its socket.

A fierce gust leaped against the outer face of the door and thrust in upon it, striving to burst it bodily from its bearings. The top and the free side of the bottom bowed in. But the branches were still green and tough, the bamboo like whalebone, and the shrunken creepers held the frame together as though the joints were lashed with wire rope. Failing to smash in the elastic structure, or to snap the crossbar, it were as if the blast flung itself alternately against the top and bottom in a fierce attempt to again whirl the frame about. The white glare streaming in through the interstices showed the girl her opportunity. She grasped another bar and shot it into its socket as the lower part of the door gave back with the shifting of the pressure to the top. It was then a simple matter to slide the remaining bars into the deep-sunk holes. Within half a minute she had made the door fast, from the first bar to the sixth.

A heavy spray was beating in upon her through the chinks of the framework. She drew back and sought shelter in a niche at the side. Narrow as was the slit above the top of the door, it let in a torrent of water, which spouted clear across and against the far wall of the cave. It gushed down upon her bed and was already flooding the cave floor.

She piled higher the cocoanuts stored in her niche, and perched herself upon the heap to keep above the water. But even in her sheltered corner the eddying wind showered her with spray. She waded across for her skin-covered sunshade, and returned to huddle beneath it, in the still misery and terror of a hunted animal that has crept wounded into a hole.

During the first hurricane there had been companions to whom she could look for help and comfort, and she had been to a degree unaware of the greatness of the danger. But in the few short weeks since, she had caught more than one glimpse of Primeval Nature,—she of the bloody fang, blind, remorseless, insensate, destroying, ever destroying.

True, this was on solid land, while before there had been the peril of the sea. But now the girl was alone. Outside the straining walls of her refuge, the hurricane yelled and shrieked and roared,—a headless, formless monster, furious to burst in upon her, to overthrow her stanch old tree giant, that in his fall his shattered trunk might crush and mangle her. Or at any instant a thunder-bolt might rend open the great tower of living wood, and hurl her blackened body into the pool on the cave floor.

Once she fancied that she heard Blake shouting outside the door; but when she screamed a shrill response, the blast mocked her with echoing shrieks, and she dared not venture to free the door. If it were Blake, he did not shout again. After a time she began to think that the sound had been no more than a freak of the shifting wind. Yet the thought of him out in the full fury of the cyclone served to turn her thoughts from her own danger. She prayed aloud for his safety, beseeching her God that he be spared. She sought to pray even for Winthrope. But the vision of that beastly face rose up before her, and she could not—then.

Presently she became aware of a change in the storm. The terrific gusts blew with yet greater violence, the thunder crashed heavier, the lightning filled the air with a flame of dazzling white light. But the rain no longer gushed across on the spot where her bed had been. It was entering at a different angle, and its force was broken by the bend in the thick wall of the entrance. After a time the deluge dashed aslant the entrance, gushing down the door in a cataract of foam.

Another interval, and the driving downpour no longer struck even the edge of the opening. The wind was veering rapidly as the cyclone centre moved past on one side. The area of the hurricane was little more than thrice that of a tornado, and it was advancing along its course at great speed. An hour more, and the outermost rim of the huge whirl was passing over the cleft.

Quickly the hurricane gusts fell away to a gale; the gale became a breeze; the breeze lulled and died away, stifled by the torrential rain.

Within the baobab all was again dark and silent. Utterly exhausted, the girl had sunk back against the friendly wall of the tree, and fallen asleep.

She was wakened by a hoarse call: "Miss Jenny! Miss Jenny, answer me! Are you all right?"

She started up, barely saving herself from a fall as the big unhusked nuts rolled beneath her feet. The morning sunlight was streaming in over her door. She sprang down ankle-deep into the mire of the cave floor, and ran to loosen the bars. As the door swung up, she darted out, with a cry of delight: "You are safe—safe! Oh, I was so afraid for you! But you're drenched! You must build a fire—dry yourself—at once!"

"Wait," said Blake. "I've got to tell you something."

He caught her outstretched hands, and pushed them down with gentle force. His face was grave, almost solemn.

"Think you can stand bad news—a shock?"

"I— What is it? You look so strange!"

"It's about Winthrope,—something very bad—"

She turned, with a gasp, and hid her face in her hands, shuddering with horror and loathing.

"Oh! oh!" she cried, "I know already—I know all!"

"All?" demanded Blake, staring blankly.

"Yes; all! And—and he made me think it was you!" She gasped, and fell silent.

Blake's face went white. He spoke in a clear, vibrant voice, tense as an overstrained violin string: "I am speaking about Winthrope—understand me?—Winthrope. He has been badly hurt."

"The door swung down and struck him, when he was creeping in."

"God!" roared Blake. "I picked him up like a sick baby—the beast!—'stead of grinding my heel in his face! God! I'll—"

"Tom! don't—don't even speak it! Tom!"

"God! When a helpless girl—when a —!" He choked, beside himself with rage.

She sprang to him, and caught his sleeve in a convulsive grasp. "Hush, for mercy's sake! Tom Blake, remember—you're a man!"

He calmed like a ferocious dog at the voice of its master; but it was several minutes before he could bring himself to obey her insistent urging that he should return to the injured man.

"I'll go," he at last growled. "Wouldn't do it even for you, but he's good as dead—lucky for him!"

"Dead!"

"Dying. . . . . You stay away."

He went around the baobab and a few paces along the cleft to the place where a limp form lay huddled on the ledges, out of the mud. Slowly, as though drawn by the fascination of horror, the girl crept after him. When she saw the broken, storm-beaten thing that had been Winthrope, she stopped, and would have turned back. After all, as Blake had said, he was dying—

When she stood at the feet of the writhing figure, and looked down into the battered face, it required all her will-power to keep from fainting. Blake frowned up at her for an instant, but said nothing.

Winthrope was speaking, feebly and brokenly, yet distinctly: "Really, I did not mean any harm—at first—you know. But a man does not always have control—"

"Not a beast like you!" growled Blake.

"Ow! Don't 'it me! I say now, I'm done for! My legs are cold already—"

"Oh, quick, Mr. Blake! build a fire! It may be, some hot broth—"

"Too late," muttered Blake. "See here, Winthrope, there's no use lying about it. You're going out mighty soon. See if you can't die like a man."

"Die! . . . Gawd, but I can't die—I can't die—Ow! it burns!"

He flung up a hand, and sought to tear at his wounds.

"Hold hard!" cried Blake, catching the hand in an iron grip.

Something in his touch, or the tone of command, seemed to cower the wretched man into a state of abject submission.

"S'elp me, I'll confess!—I'll confess all!" he babbled. "The stones are sewed in the stomach pad; I 'ad to take 'em hout of their settings, and melt up the gold." He paused, and a cunning smile stole over his distorted features. "Ho, wot a bloomin' lark! Valet plays the gent, an' they never 'as a hinkling! Mr. Cecil Winthrope, hif you please, an' a 'int of a title—wot a lark! 'Awkings, me lad, you're a gay 'oaxer! Wot a lark! wot a lark!"

Again there was a pause. The breath of the wounded man came in labored gasps. There was an ominous rattling in his throat. Yet once again he rallied, and this time his eyes turned to Miss Leslie, bright with an agonized consciousness of her presence and of all his guilt and shame.

His voice shrilled out in quavering appeal: "Don't—don't look at me, miss! I tried to make myself a gentleman; God knows I tried! I fought my way up out of the East End—out of that hell—and none ever lifted finger to help me. I educated myself like a scholar—then the stock sharks cheated me of my savings—out of the last penny; and I had to take service. My God! a valet—his Grace's valet, and I a scholar! Do you wonder the devil got into me? Do you—"

Blake's deep voice, firm but strangely husky, broke in upon and silenced the cry of agony: "There, I guess you've said enough."

"Enough!—and last night—My God! to be such a beast! The devil tempted me—aye, and he's paid me out in my own coin! I'm done for! God ha' mercy on me!—God ha' mercy—"

Again came the gasping rattle; this time there was no rally.

Blake thrust himself between Miss Leslie and the crumpled figure.

"Get back around the tree," he said harshly.

"What are you going to do?"

"That's my business," he replied. He thrust his burning-glass into her hand. "Here; go and build a fire, if you can find any dry stuff."

"You're not going to— You'll bury him!"

"Yes. Whatever he may have been, he's dead now, poor devil!"

"I can't go," she half whispered, "not until—until I've learned— Do you—can you tell me just what is paranoia?"

Blake studied a little, and tapped the top of his head.

"Near as I can say, it's softening of the brain.—up there."

"Do you think that—" she hesitated—"that he had it?"

Again Blake paused to consider.

"Well, I'm no alienist. I thought him a softy from the first. But that was all in line with what he was playing on us—British dude. Fooled me, and I'd been chumming with Jimmy Scarbridge,—and Jimmy was the straight goods, fresh imported—monocle even—when I first ran up against him. No; this—this Hawkins, if that's his name, had brains all right. Still, he may have been cracked. When folks go dotty, they sometimes get extra 'cute. The best I can think of him is that losing his savings may have made him slip a cog, and then the scare over the way we landed here and his spells of fever probably hurried up the softening."

"Then you believe his story?"

"Yes, I do. But if you'll go, please."

"One thing more—I must know now! Do you remember the day when you set up the signal, and you—you quarrelled with him?"

Blake reddened, and dropped his gaze. "Did he go and tell you that? The sneak!"

"If you please, let us say nothing more about him. But would you care to tell me what you meant—what you said then?"

Blake's flush deepened; but he raised his head, and faced her squarely as he answered: "No; I'm not going to repeat any dead man's talk; and as for what I said, this isn't the time or place to say anything in that line—now that we're alone. Understand?"

"I'm afraid I do not, Mr. Blake. Please explain."

"Don't ask me, Miss Jenny. I can't tell you now. You'll have to wait till we get aboard ship. We'll catch a steamer before long. 'T isn't every one of them that goes ashore in these blows."

"Why did you build that door? Did you suspect—" She glanced down at the huddled figure between them.

Blake frowned and hesitated; then burst out almost angrily: "Well, you know now he was a sneak; so it's not blabbing to tell that much—I knew he was before; and it's never safe to trust a sneak."

"Thank you!" she said, and she turned away quickly that she might not again look at the prostrate figure.

CHAPTER XXI

WRECKAGE AND SALVAGE

All the wood in the cleft was sodden from the fierce downpour that had accompanied the cyclone; all the cleft bottom other than the bare ledges was a bed of mud; everything without the tree-cave had been either blown away or heaped with broken boughs and mud-spattered rubbish. But the girl had far too much to think about to feel any concern over the mere damage and destruction of things. It was rather a relief to find something that called for work.

Not being able to find dry fuel, she gathered a quantity of the least sodden of the twigs and branches, and spread them out on a ledge in the clear sunshine. While her firewood was drying, she scraped away the mud and litter heaped upon her rude hearth. She then began a search for lost articles. When she dug out the pottery ware, she found her favorite stew-pot and one of the platters in fragments. The drying-frames for the meat had been blown away, and so had the antelope and hyena skins.

Catching sight of a bit of white down among the bamboos, she went to it, and was not a little surprised to see the tattered remnant of her duck skirt. It had evidently been torn from the signal staff by the first gust of the cyclone, whirled down into the cleft by some flaw or eddy in the wind, and wadded so tightly into the heart of the thick clump of stems that all the fury of the storm had failed to dislodge it. Its recovery seemed to the girl a special providence; for of course they must keep up a signal on the cliff.

Having started her fire and set on a stew, she hunted out her sewing materials from their crevice in the cave, and began mending the slits in the torn flag. While she worked she sat on a shaded ledge, her bare feet toasting in the sun, and her soggy, mud-smeared moccasins drying within reach. When Blake appeared, the moccasins were still where she had first set them; but the little pink feet were safely tucked up beneath the tattered flag. Fortunately, the sight of the white cloth prevented Blake from noticing the moccasins.

"Hello!" he exclaimed. "What's that?—the flag? Say, that's luck! I'll break out a bamboo right off. Old staff's carried clean away."

"Mr. Blake,—just a moment, please. What have you done with—with it?"

Blake jerked his thumb upward.

"You have carried him up on the cliff?"

"Best place I could think of. No animals—and I piled stones over.... But, I say, look here."

He drew out a piece of wadded cloth, marked off into little squares by crossing lines of stitches. One of the squares near the edge had been ripped open. Blake thrust in his finger, and worked out an emerald the size of a large pea.

"O-h-h!" cried Miss Leslie, as he held the glittering gem out to her in his rough palm.

He drew it back, and carefully thrust it again into its pocket.

"That's one," he said. "There's another in every square of this innocent, harmless rag—dozens of them. He must have made a clean sweep of the duke's—or, more like, the duchess's jewels. Now, if you please, I want you to sew this up tight again, and—"

"I cannot—I cannot touch it!" she cried.

"Say, I didn't mean to— It was confounded stupid of me," mumbled Blake. "Won't you excuse me?"

"Of course! It was only the—the thought that—"

"No wonder. I always am a fool when it comes to ladies. I'll fix the thing all right."

Catching up the nearest small pot, he crammed the quilted cloth down within it, and filled it to the brim with sticky mud.

"There! Guess nobody's going to run off with a jug of mud—and it won't hurt the stones till we get a chance to look up the owner. He won't be hard to find—English duke minus a pint of first-class sparklers! Will you mind its setting in the cave after things are fixed up?"

"No; not as it is."

He nodded soberly. "All right, then. Now I'll go for the new flag-staff. You might set out breakfast."

She nodded in turn, and when he came back from the bamboos with the largest of the great canes on his shoulder, his breakfast was waiting for him. She set it before him, and turned to go again to her sewing.

"Hold on," he said. "This won't do. You've got to eat your share."

"I do not—I am not hungry."

"That's no matter. Here!"

He forced upon her a bowl of hot broth, and she drank it because she could not resist his rough kindness.

"Good! Now a piece of meat," he said.

143

"Please, Mr. Blake!" she protested.

"Yes, you must!"

She took a bite, and sought to eat; but there was such a lump in her throat that she could not swallow. The tears gushed into her eyes, and she began to weep.

Blake's close-set lips relaxed, and he nodded.

"That's it; let it run out. You're overwrought. There's nothing like a good cry to ease off a woman's nerves—and I guess ladies aren't much different from women when it comes to such things."

"But I—I want to get the flag mended!" she sobbed.

"All right, all right; plenty of time!" he soothed. "I'm going to see how things look down the cleft."

He bolted the last of his meat, and at once left her alone to cry herself back to calmness over the stitching of the signal.

His first concern was for the barricade. As he had feared, he found that it had been blown to pieces. The greater part of the thorn branches which he had gathered with so much labor were scattered to the four corners of the earth. He stood staring at the wreckage in glum silence; but he did not swear, as he would have done the week before. Presently his face cleared, and he began to whistle in a plaintive minor key. He was thinking of how she had looked when she darted out of the tree at his call—of her concern for him. When he was so angered at Winthrope, she had called him Tom!

After a time he started on, picking his way over the remnant of the barricade, without a falter in his whistling. The deluge of rain had poured down the cleft in a torrent, tearing away the root-matted soil and laying bare the ledges in the channel of the spring rill. But aside from an occasional boggy hole, the water had drained away.

At the foot, about the swollen pool, was a wide stretch of rubbish and mud. He worked his way around the edge, and came out on the plain, where the sandy soil was all the firmer for its drenching. He swung away at a lively clip. The air was fresh and pure after the storm, and a slight breeze tempered the sun-rays.

He kept on along the cliff until he turned the point. It was not altogether advisable to bathe at this time of day; but he had been caught out by the cyclone in a corner of the swamp, across the river, where the soil was of clay. Only his anxiety for Miss Leslie had enabled him to fight his way out of the all but impassable morass which the storm deluge had made of the half-dry swamp. At dawn he had reached the river, and swam across, reckless of the crocodiles. The turbid water of the stream had rid him of only part of his accumulated slime and ooze. So now he washed out his tattered garments as well as he could without soap, and while they were drying on the sun-scorched rocks, swam about in the clear, tonic sea-water, quite as reckless of the sharks as he had been of the ugly crocodiles in the river.

For all this, he was back at the baobab before Miss Leslie had stitched up the last slit in the torn flag.

She looked up at him, with a brave attempt at a smile.

"I am afraid I'm not much of a needle-woman," she sighed. "Look at those stitches!"

"Don't fret. They'll hold all right, and that's what we want," he reassured her. "Give it me, now. I've got to get it up, and hurry back for a nap. No sleep last night—I was out beyond the river, in the swamp—and to-night I'll have to go on watch. The barricade is down."

"Oh, that is too bad! Couldn't I take a turn on watch?"

Blake shook his head. "No; I'll sleep to-day, and work rebuilding the barricade to-night. Toward morning I might build up the fire, and take a nap."

He caught up the flag and its new staff, and swung away through the cleft.

He returned much sooner than Miss Leslie expected, and at once began to throw up a small lean-to of bamboos over a ledge at the cliff foot, behind the baobab. The girl thought he was making himself a hut, in place of the canopy under which he had slept before the storm, which, like Winthrope's, had been carried away. But when he stopped work, he laconically informed her that all she had to do to complete her new house was to dry some leaves.

"But I thought it was for yourself!" she protested. "I will sleep inside the tree."

"Doc Blake says no!" he rejoined—"not till it's dried out."

She glanced at his face, and replied, without a moment's hesitancy: "Very well. I will do what you think best."

"That's good," he said, and went at once to lie down for his much needed sleep.

He awoke just soon enough before dark to see the results of her hard day's labor. All the provisions stored in the tree had been brought out to dry, and a great stack of fuel, ready for burning, was piled up against the baobab; while all about the tree the rubbish had been neatly gathered together in heaps. Blake looked his admiration for her industry. But then his forehead wrinkled.

"You oughtn't to've done so much," he admonished.

"I'll show you I can tote fair!" she rejoined. During the afternoon she had called to mind that odd expression of a Southern girl chum, and had been waiting her opportunity to banter him with it.

He stared at her open-eyed, and laughed.

"Say, Miss Jenny, you'd better look out. You'll be speaking American, first thing!"

Thereupon, they fell to chattering like children out of school, each happy to be able to forget for the moment that broken figure up on the cliff top and the haunting fear of what another day might bring to them.

When they had eaten their meal, both with keen appetites, Blake sprang up, with a curt "Good-night!" and swung off down the cleft. The girl looked after him, with a lingering smile.

"I wish he hadn't rushed off so suddenly," she murmured. "I was just going to thank him for—for everything!"

The color swept over her face in a deep blush, and she darted around to her tiny hut as though some one might have overheard her whisper.

Yet, after all, she had said nothing; or, at least, she had merely said "everything."

CHAPTER XXII

UNDERSTANDING AND MISUNDERSTANDING

In the morning she found Blake scraping energetically at the inner surfaces of a pair of raw hyena skins.

"So you've killed more game!" she exclaimed.

"Game? No; hyenas. I hated to waste good poison on the brutes; but nothing else showed up, and I need a new pair of pa–er–trousers."

"Was it not dangerous–great beasts like these!"

"Not even enough to make it interesting. I'd have had some fun, though, with that confounded lion when the moon came up, if he hadn't sneaked off into the grass."

"A lion?"

"Yes. Didn't you hear him? The skulking brute prowled around for hours before the moon rose, when it was pitch dark. It was mighty lonesome, with him yowling down by the pool. Half a chance, and I'd given him something to yowl about. But it wasn't any use firing off my arrows in the dark, and, as I said, he sneaked off before–"

"Tom–Mr. Blake!–you must not risk your life!"

"Don't you worry about me. I've learned how to look out for Tom Blake. And you can just bank on it I'm going to look out for Miss Jenny Leslie, too! . . . . But say, after breakfast, suppose we take a run out on the cliffs for eggs?"

"I do not wish any to-day, thank you."

He waited a little, studying her down-bent face.

"Well," he muttered; "you don't have to come. I know I oughtn't to take a moment's time. I did quite a bit last night; but if you think–"

She glanced up, puzzled. His meaning flashed upon her, and she rose.

"Oh, not that! I will come," she answered, and hastened to prepare the morning meal.

When they came to the tree-ladder, she found that the heap of stones built up by Blake to facilitate the first part of the ascent was now so high that she could climb into the branches without difficulty. She surmised that Blake had found it necessary to build up the pile before he could ascend with his burden.

They were at the foot of the heap, when, with a sharp exclamation, Blake sprang up into the branches, and scrambled to the top in hot haste. Wondering what this might mean, Miss Leslie followed as fast as she could. When she reached the top, she saw him running across towards an out-jutting point on the north edge of the cliff.

She had hurried after him for more than half the distance before she perceived the vultures that were gathered in a solemn circle about a long and narrow heap of stones, on a ledge, down on the sloping brink of the cliff. While at the foot of the tree Blake had seen one of the grewsome flock descending to join the others, and, fearful of what might be happening, had rushed on ahead.

At his approach, the croaking watchers hopped awkwardly from the ledges, and soared away; only to wheel, and circle back overhead. Miss Leslie shrank down, shuddering. Blake came back near her, and began to gather up the pieces of loose rock which were strewn about beneath the ledges on that part of the cliff.

"I know I piled up enough," he explained, in response to her look. "All the same, a few more will do no harm."

"Then you are sure those awful birds have not—"

"Yes; I'm sure."

He carried an armful of rocks to lay on the mound. When he began to gather more, she followed his example. They worked in silence, piling the rough stones gently one upon another, until the cairn had grown to twice its former size. The air on the open cliff top was fresher than in the cleft, and Miss Leslie gave little heed to the absence of shade. She would have worked on under the burning sun without thought of consequences. But Blake knew the need of moderation.

"There; that'll do," he said. "He may have been—all he was; but we've no more than done our duty. Now, we'll stroll out on the point."

"I should prefer to return."

"No doubt. But it's time you learned how to go nesting. What if you should be left alone here? Besides, it looks to me like the signal is tearing loose."

She accompanied him out along the cliff crest until they stood in the midst of the bird colony, half deafened by their harsh clamor. She had never ventured into their concourse when alone. Even now she cried out, and would have retreated before the sharp bills and beating wings had not Blake walked ahead and kicked the squawking birds out of the path. Having made certain that the big white flag was still secure on its staff, he led the way along the seaward brink of the cliff, pointing out the different kinds of seafowl, and shouting information about such of their habits and qualities as were of concern to hungry castaways.

148

He concluded the lesson by descending a dizzy flight of ledges to rob the nest of a frigate bird. It was a foolhardy feat at best, and doubly so in view of the thousands of eggs lying all around in the hollows of the cliff top. But from these Blake had recently culled out all the fresh settings of the frigate birds, and none of the other eggs equalled them in delicacy of flavor.

"How's that?" he demanded, as he drew himself up over the edge of the cliff, and handed the big chalky-white egg into her keeping.

"I would rather go without than see you take such risks," she replied coldly.

"You would, eh!" he cried, quite misunderstanding her, and angered by what seemed to him a gratuitous rebuff. "Well, I'd rather you'd say nothing than speak in that tone. If you don't want the egg heave it over."

Unable to conceive any cause for his sudden anger, she was alarmed, and drew back, watching him with sidelong glances.

"What's the matter?" he demanded. "Think I'm going to bite you?"

She shrank farther away, and did not answer. He stared at her, his eyes hard and bright. Suddenly he burst into a harsh laugh, and strode away towards the cliff, savagely kicking aside the birds that came in his path.

When, an hour later, the girl crept back along the cleft to the baobab, she saw him hard at work building a little hut, several yards down towards the barricade. The moment she perceived what he was about her bearing became less guarded, and she took up her own work with a spirit and energy which she had not shown since the adventure with the puff adder.

At her call to the noon meal, Blake took his time to respond, and when he at last came to join her, he was morose and taciturn. She met him with a smile, and exerted all her womanly tact to conciliate him.

"You must help me eat the egg," she said. "I've boiled it hard."

"Rather eat beef," he mumbled.

"But just to please me—when I've cooked it your way!"

He uttered an inarticulate sound which she chose to interpret as assent. The egg was already shelled. She cut it exactly in half, and served one of the pieces to him with a bit of warm fat and a pinch of salt. As he took the dish, he raised his sullen eyes to her face. She met his gaze with a look of smiling insistence.

"Come now," she said; "please don't refuse. I'm sorry I was so rude."

"Well, if you feel that way about it!—not that I care for fancy dishes," he responded gruffly.

"It would be missing half the enjoyment to eat such a delicacy without some one to share it," she said.

Blake looked away without answer. But she could see that his face was beginning to clear. Greatly encouraged, she chatted away as though they were seated at her father's dinner-table, and he was an elderly friend from the business world whom it was her duty to entertain.

For a while Blake betrayed little interest, confining himself to monosyllables except when he commented on the care with which she had cooked the various dishes. When she least expected, he looked up at her, his lips parted in a broad smile. She stopped short, for she had been describing her first social triumphs, and his untimely levity embarrassed her.

"Don't get mad, Miss Jenny," he said, his eyes twinkling. "You don't know how funny it seems to sit here and listen to you talking about those things. It's like serving up ice cream and onions in the same dish."

"I'm sure, Mr. Blake—"

"Beats a burlesque all hollow—Mrs. Sint-Regis-Waldoff's chop-sooey tea and young Mrs. Vandam-Jones's auto-cotillon—with us sitting here like troglodytes, chewing snake-poisoned antelope, and you in that Kundry dress—"

"Do you—I was not aware that you knew about music."

"Don't know a note. But give me a chance to hear good music, and I'm there, if I have to stand in the peanut gallery."

"Oh, I'm so glad! I'm very, very fond of music! Have you been to Bayreuth?"

"Where's that?"

"In Germany. It is where his operas are given as staged by Wagner himself. It is indescribably grand and inspiring—above all, the Parsifal!"

"I'll most certainly take that in, even if I have to cut short my engagement in this gee-lorious clime—not but what, when it comes to leopard ladies—" He paused, and surveyed her with frank admiration.

The blood leaped into her face.

"Oh!" she gasped, "I never dreamed that even such a man as you would compare me with—with a creature like that!"

"Such a man as me!" repeated Blake, staring. "What do you mean? I know I'm not much of a ladies' man; but to be yanked up like this when a fellow is trying to pay a compliment—well, it's not just what you'd call pleasant."

"I beg your pardon, Mr. Blake. I misunderstood. I—"

"That's all right, Miss Jenny! I don't ask any lady to beg my pardon. The only thing is I don't see why you should flare out at me that way."

For a full minute she sat, with down-bent head, her face clouded with doubt and indecision. At last she bravely raised her eyes to meet his.

"Do you wonder that I am not quite myself?" she asked. "You should remember that I have always had the utmost comforts of life, and have been cared for— Don't you see how terrible it is for me? And then the death of—of—"

"I can't be sorry for that!"

"But even you felt how terrible it was . . . . and then—Oh, surely, you must see how—how embarrassing—"

It was Blake's turn to look down and hesitate. She studied his face, her bosom heaving with quick-drawn breath; but she could make nothing of his square jaw and firm-set lips. His eyes were concealed by the brim of his leaf hat. When he spoke, seemingly it was to change the subject: "Guess you saw me making my hut. I'm fixing it so it'll do me even when it rains."

Had he been the kind of man that she had been educated to consider as alone entitled to the name of gentleman, she could have felt certain that he had intended the remark for a delicately worded assurance. But was Tom Blake, for all his blunt kindliness, capable of such tact? She chose to consider that he was.

"It's a cunning little bungalow. But will not the rain flood you out?"

"It's going to have a raised floor. You're more like to have the rain drive in on you again. I'll have to rig up a porch over your door. It won't do to stuff up the hole. You've little enough air as it is. But that can wait a while. There's other work more pressing. First, there's the barricade. By the time that's done, those hyena skins will be cured enough to use. I've got to have new trousers soon, and new shoes, too."

"I can do the sewing, if you will cut out the pattern."

"No; I'll take a stagger at it myself first. I'd rather you'd go egging. You need to run around more, to keep in trim."

"I feel quite well now, and I am growing so strong! The only thing is this constant heat."

"We'll have to grin and bear it. After all, it's not so bad, if only we can stave off the fever. Another reason I want you to go for eggs is that you can take your time about it, and keep a look-out for steamers."

"Then you think –?"

"Don't screw up your hopes too high. We've little show of being picked up by a chance boat on a coast with reefs like this. But I figure that if I was in your daddy's shoes, it'd be high time for me to be cabling a ship to run up from Natal, or down from Zanzibar, to look around for jettison, et cetera."

"I'm sure papa will offer a big reward."

"Second the motion! I've a sort of idea I wouldn't mind coming in for a reward myself."

"You? Oh, yes; to be sure. Papa is generous, and he will be grateful to any one who—"

"You think I mean his dirty money!" broke in Blake, hotly.

Her confusion told him that he had not been mistaken. His face, only a moment since bright and pleasant, took on its sullenest frown.

Miss Leslie rose hurriedly, and started along the cleft.

"Hello!" he called. "Not going for eggs now, are you?"

She did not reply.

"Hang it all, Miss Jenny! Don't go off like that."

"May I ask you to excuse me, Mr. Blake? Is that sufficient?"

"Sufficient? It's enough to give a fellow a chill! Come now; don't go off mad. You know I've a quick temper. Can't you make allowances?"

"You've—you've no right to look so angry, even if I did misunderstand you. You misunderstood me!" She caught herself up with a half sob. His silence gave her time to recover her composure. She continued with excessive politeness, "Need I repeat my request to be excused, Mr. Blake?"

"No; once is enough! But honest now, I didn't mean to be nasty."

"Good-day, Mr. Blake."

"Oh, da-darn it, good-day!" he groaned.

When, a few minutes later, she returned, he was gone. He did not come back until some time after dark, when she had withdrawn to her lean-to for the night. His hands were bleeding from thorn scratches; but after a hasty supper, he went back down the cleft to build up the new wall of the barricade with the great stack of fresh thorn-brush that he had gathered during the afternoon.

CHAPTER XXIII

THE END OF THE WORLD

In the morning he met Miss Leslie with a sullen bearing, which, however, did not altogether conceal his desire to be on friendly terms. Having regained her self-control, she responded to this with such tact that by evening each felt more at ease in the new relationship, and Blake had lost every trace of his moroseness. The fact that both were passionately fond of music proved an immense help. It gave them an impersonal source of mutual sympathy and understanding,—a common meeting-ground in the world of art and culture, apart from and above the plane of their material wants.

Yet for all his enjoyment of the girl's wide knowledge of everything relating to music, Blake took care that their talks and discussions did not interfere with the activities of their primitive mode of life. As soon as he had finished with the barricade, he devoted himself to his tailoring and shoe-making; while Miss Leslie, between her cooking and wood-gathering and daily visits to the cliff for eggs, had much to occupy both her thoughts and her hands.

At first every ascent of the cliff was embittered by a painful consciousness of the cairn upon the north edge. Fortunately it was not in sight from the direct path to the headland, and, as she refrained from visiting it, the new happenings of her wild life soon thrust Winthrope and his death out of the foreground of her thoughts. Each day she had to nerve herself to meet the beaks and wings of the despoiled nest-owners; each day she looked with greater hope for the expected rescue ship, only to be increasingly disappointed.

But the hours she spent on the cliff crest after gathering the day's supply of eggs were not spent merely in watching and longing. The inconvenience of carrying the eggs in a handkerchief or in one of the heavy jars suggested a renewal of her attempt at basket-making. Memory, perseverance, and a trace of inventiveness enabled her to produce a small but serviceable hamper of split bamboo.

Encouraged by this success she gathered a quantity of tough, wiry grass, and wove a hat to take the place of the flimsy palm-leaf makeshift. The result was by no means satisfactory with regard to style, its shape being intermediate between a Mexican sombrero and a funnel; but aside from its appearance, she could not have wished for a more comfortable head-cover. Before showing it to Blake, she wove a second one for him, so that they were able to cast aside the grotesque, palm-leaf affairs at the same time.

The following morning Blake appeared in an outfit to match her leopard-skin dress. He had singed off the hair of the hide out of which he had made his moccasins, and his hyena-skin trousers quite matched the bristling stubble on his face.

"Hey, Miss Jenny!" he hailed; "what d' you think of this for fancy needlework?"

"Splendid! You're the very picture of an Argentine vaquero."

"Greaser?—ugh! Let me get back to the Weary Willy pants!"

"I mean you are very picturesque."

"That's it, is it? Glad I've got something to call your leopardine gown that won't make you huffy."

"We can at least call our costumes serviceable, and mine has proved much cooler than I expected."

"But our new hats beat all for that—regular sunshades. What do you say?—there's a good breeze— Let's take a hike."

"Not to the river! The very thought of that dreadful snake—"

"No; just the other way. I've been thinking for some time that we ought to run down to that south headland, and take a squint at the coast beyond. Ten to one, it's another stretch of swamps, but—"

"You think there is a chance we may find a town?"

"About one chance in a million, even for a native village. The slave trade wiped the niggers off this coast, and I guess those that hit out upcountry ran so hard they haven't been able to get back yet."

"But it has been years since the slave trade was forbidden."

"And they don't sell beer in Kansas—oh, no! I'll bet the dhows still slip over from Madagascar when the moon is in the right quarter. At any rate, niggers are mighty scarce or mighty shy around here. I've kept a watch for smoke, and haven't seen a suspicion of it anywhere. Maybe the swamps swing around inland and cut off this strip of coast. It looked that way to me when I made that trip along the ridge. But there's a chance it used to be inhabited, and we may run across an abandoned village."

"I do not see that the discovery would do us any good."

"How about the chance of grain or bananas still growing? But that's all a guess. We're going because we need a change."

She nodded, and hastened to prepare breakfast, while he packed a skin bag with food, and examined the slender tips of his arrows. As a matter of precaution, he had been keeping them in the cigarette case, where the points would be certain of a coat of the sticky poison and at the same time guarded against inflicting a chance wound. But as he was now about to set out on a journey, he fitted tips into the heads of his two straightest shafts.

The morning was still fresh when they closed the barricade behind them and descended to the pool. There was no game in sight, but Blake had no wish to hunt at the commencement of the trip. The steady southwest wind had blown the sky clear of its malarial haze, and gave promise of a day which should know nothing of sultry calm—a day on which game would be hard to stalk, but one perfectly suited for a long tramp.

Mindful of ticks, Blake headed obliquely across to the beach. Once on the smooth, hard sand, they swung along at a brisk pace, light-hearted and keen with the spirit of adventure. Never had they felt more companionable. Miss Leslie laughed and chatted and sang snatches of songs, while Blake beat time with his club, or sought to whistle grand opera—he had healed his blistered lips some time before by liberal applications of antelope tallow.

Gulls and terns circled about them, or hovered over the water, ready to swoop down upon their finny prey. Sandpipers ran along the beach within a stone's throw, but the curlews showed their greater knowledge of mankind by keeping beyond gunshot.

Once a great flock of geese drove high overhead, their leader honking the alarm as they swept above the suspicious figures on the beach. Like the curlews, they had knowledge of mankind. But the flock of white pelicans which came sailing along in stately leisure on their immense wings floated past so low that Blake felt certain he could shoot one. He raised his bow and took aim, but refrained from shooting, at the thought that it might be a sheer waste of his precious poison.

A little later a herd of large animals appeared on the border of the grass jungle, but wheeled and dashed back into cover so quickly that Blake barely had time to make out that they were buffaloes—the first he had seen on this coast, but easily recognized by their resemblance to the Cape variety. Their flight gave him small concern; for the time being he was more interested in topography than game.

The southern headland now lay close before them, its seaward face rearing up sheer and lofty, but the approach behind running down in broken terraces. Mid-morning found the explorers at the foot of the ridge. Blake squinted up at the boulder-strewn slopes and the crannies of the broken ledges.

"Likely place for snakes, Miss Jenny," he remarked. "Guess I'd better lead."

Eager as she was to look over into the country beyond, the girl dropped into second place, and made no complaint about the wary slowness of her companion's advance. She found the most difficult parts of the ascent quite easy after her training on the tree-ladder. Blake could have taken ledges and all at a run, but as he mounted each terrace, he halted to spy out the ground before him. Like Miss Leslie, he was looking for snakes, though for an exactly opposite reason. He wished to add to the contents of the cigarette case.

Greatly to his disappointment and the girl's relief, neither snake nor sign of snake was to be seen all the way up the ridge. As they neared the crest Blake turned to offer her his hand up the last ledges, and in the instant they gained the top.

The wind, now freshening to a gale, struck the girl with such force that she would have been blown back down the ledges had not Blake clutched her wrist. Heedless alike of the painful grip which held her and of the gusts which tore at her skirt, the girl stood gazing out across the desolate swamps which stretched away to the southwest as far as the eye could see. She did not speak until Blake led her down behind the shelter of the crest ledges.

"What's the matter?" he demanded. "Didn't I warn you?"

She looked away to hide the tears which sprang into her eyes.

"I can't explain—only, it makes me feel so—so lonely!"

"Oh, come now, little woman; don't take on so!" he urged. "It might be a lot worse, you know. We've gotten along pretty well, considering."

"You have been very kind, Mr. Blake, and as you say, matters might have been worse. I do not forget how far more terrible was our situation the morning after the storm. Yet you must realize how disappointing it is to lose even the slightest hope of escape."

"Well, I don't know. If it wasn't for the fever that's bound to come with the rains, I, for one, would just as leave stick to this camp right along, providing the company don't change."

She turned upon him with flashing eyes, all thought of caution lost in her anger. "How dare you say such a thing? You are contemptible! I despise you!"

"My, Miss Jenny, but you are pretty when you get mad!" he exclaimed.

The answer took her completely aback. He was neither angry nor laughing at her, but met her defiant glance with candid, sober admiration. There was something more than admiration in his glowing eyes; yet she could not but see that her alarm had been baseless. His manner had never been more respectful. Suddenly she found that she could no longer meet his gaze. She looked away and stammered lamely, "You—you shouldn't say such things, you know."

"Why not? Hasn't everything been running smooth the last few days? Haven't we been good chummy comrades? Of course you've got the worst of the deal. I know I'm not much on fancy talk; but I like to hear it when I've a chance. I've led a lonesome sort of life since they did for my sisters— No; I'm not going to rake that up again. I'm only trying to give you an idea what it means to a fellow to be with a lady like you. May be it isn't polite to tell you all this, but it's just what I feel, and I never did amount to shucks as a liar."

"I believe I understand you, Mr. Blake, and I really feel highly complimented."

"No, you don't, any such thing, Miss Jenny. Own up, now! If I met you to-morrow on your papa's doorstep, you'd cut me cold."

"I should if you continued to be so rude. Have you no regard for my feelings? But here we are, talking nonsense, when we should be going—"

"Is it nonsense?" he broke in. "What does life mean, anyway? Here we can be true friends and comrades,—real, free living people. It can't be that you want to go back to all those society shams, after you've seen real life! As for me, what have I to gain by going back to the everlasting grind? I don't mind work; but when a man has nothing ahead to work for but a bank account, when it's grind, grind, grind till your head goes stale and all the world looks black, then there's no choice but throw up your job and go on a drunk, if you want to keep from a gun accident. Maybe you don't understand it. But that's what I've had to go through, time and again. Do you wonder I like to fancy an everlasting picnic here, with a little partner who wouldn't let me come within shouting distance of her in the land of lavender—trousers and peek-a-boos?"

"Mr. Blake, really you are most unjust! I could not be so—so ungrateful, after all your kindness. I—we should certainly be glad to number you among our friends."

"Drink and all, eh?"

"A man of your will-power has no need whatever to give way to such a habit."

"Course not, if he's got anything in sight worth while. Guess, though, my folks must have been poor white trash. I never could go after money just for the fun of the game. No family, no friends, no— what-you -call-it?—culture— What's the use? I have a fair head for figures; but all the mathematics that I know I've had to catch hot off the bat. It's true I grubbed my C. E. out of a correspondence school; but a fellow has to have an all-round, crack-up education to put him where it's worth while."

"You still have time to work up. You are not much over thirty."

"Twenty-seven."

"Twenty-seven! I should have thought— What a hard life you must have had!"

"Hard work? Well, I suppose Panama did do for me some. But it wasn't so much that. Few fellows could hit up the pace I've set and come out at all."

"I do not understand."

"Just what you might expect of a fellow in my fix—all kinds of gamble and drink and—the rest of it."

Miss Leslie looked away, visibly distressed. She had not been reared after the French method. Young as she was, she had fluttered at will about the borders of the garden of vice, knowing well that the gaudy blossoms were lures to entice one into the pitfall. Yet never before had she caught so clear a glimpse of the slimy depths.

"That's it!" growled Blake. "Throw me down cold, just because I'm square enough to tell you straight out. You make me tired! I'm not one of the work-ox sort, that can chew the cud all the year round, and cork the blood out of their brains. I've got to cut loose from the infernal grind once in a while, and barring a chance now and then at opera, there's never been anything but a spree—"

"Oh, but that's so dreadfully shocking, Mr. Blake!"

"And then like all the other little hypocrites, you'll go and marry one of those swell dudes who's made that sort of thing his business, and everybody knows it, but it's all politely understood to've been done sub rosa, so it's all right, because he knows how to part his name in the middle and—"

"Please, please stop, Mr. Blake! You don't know how cruel you are!"

"Cruel? Suppose I told you about the millionaire cur that— Oh, now, don't go and cry! Please don't cry, Miss Jenny! I wouldn't hurt your feelings for the world! I didn't mean anything out of the way, really I didn't! It's only that when I get to thinking of—of things, it sets me half crazy. And now, can't you see how it's going to be ten times worse for me after—with you so altogether beyond me—" He stopped short, flushed, and stammered lamely, "I—I didn't mean to say that!"

She looked down, no less embarrassed.

"Please let us talk of something else," she murmured. "It has been such a pleasant morning, until you—until we began this silly discussion."

"All right, all right! Only mop up the dewdrops, and we'll turn on the sun machine. I really didn't mean to rip out that way at all. But, you see, the thing's been rankling in me ever since we came aboard ship at the Cape, and Winthrope and Lady Bayrose had my seat changed so I couldn't see you— Not that I hold anything against them now—"

"Mr. Blake, I suppose you know that this African coast is particularly dangerous for women. So far I have escaped the fever. But you yourself said that the longer the attack is delayed, the worse it will be."

Blake's face darkened, and he turned to stare inland along the ridge. She had flicked him on the raw, and he thought that she had done so intentionally.

"You think I haven't tried—that I've been shamming!" he burst out bitterly. "You're right. There's the one chance— But I couldn't leave you till the barricade was finished, and it's been only a few days since— All the same, I oughtn't to've waited a day. I'll start it to-morrow."

"What! Start what?"

"A catamaran. I can rig one up, in short order, that, with a skin sail and an outrigger, will do fairly well to coast along inside the reefs—barring squalls. Worst thing is that it's all a guess whether the nearest settlement is up the coast or down."

"And you can think of going, and leaving me all alone here!"

"That's better than letting you risk two-to-one chances on feeding the sharks."

"But you'd be risking it!"

Blake uttered a short harsh laugh.

"What's the difference?" He paused a moment; then added, with grim humor, "Anyway, they'll have earned a meal by the time they get me chewed up."

"You sha'n't go!"

"Oh, I don't know. We'll see about it to-morrow. There's a grove of cocoanuts yonder. Come on, and I'll get some nuts. I can't see any water around here, and it would be dry eating, with only the flask."

CHAPTER XXIV

A LION LEADS THEM

The palm grove stood under the lee of the ridge, on a stretch of bare ground. Other than seaward, the open space was hemmed in by grass jungle, interspersed with clumps of thorn-brush. On the north side a jutting corner of the tall, yellow spear-grass curved out and around, with the point of the hook some fifty yards from the palms. Elsewhere the distance to the jungle was nearly twice as far.

Blake dropped the bag and his weapons, flung down his hat, and started up a palm shaft. The down-pointing bristles of his skin trousers aided his grip. Though the lofty crown of the palm was swaying in the wind, he reached the top and was down again before Miss Leslie had arranged the contents of the lunch bag.

"Guess you're not extra hungry," he remarked.

She made no response.

"Mad, eh? Well, toss me the little knife. Mine has got too good a meat-edge to spoil on these husks."

"It was very kind of you to climb for the nuts, and the wind blowing so hard up there," she said, as she handed over the penknife. "I am not angry. It is only that I feel tired and depressed. I hope I am not going to be—"

"No; you're not going to have the fever, or any such thing! You're played out, that's all. I'm a fool for bringing you so far. You'll be all right after you eat and rest. Here; drink this cocoa milk."

She drained the nut, and upon his insistence, made a pretence at eating. He was deceived until, with the satisfying of his first keen hunger, he again became observant.

"Say, that won't do!" he exclaimed. "Look at your bowl. You haven't nibbled enough to keep a mouse alive."

"Really, I am not hungry. But I am resting."

"Try another nut. I'll have one ready in two shakes."

He caught his hat, which was dragging past in a downward eddy of the wind, and weighted it with a cocoanut. He wedged another nut between his knees, and bent over it, tearing at the husk. It took him only a few moments to strip the fibre from the end and gouge open the germ hole. He held out the nut, and glanced up to meet her smile of acceptance.

She was staring past him, her eyes wide with terror, and the color fast receding from her face.

"What in— Another snake?" he demanded, twisting warily about to glare at the ground behind him.

"There—over in the grass!" she whispered, "It looked out at me with terrible, savage eyes!"

"Snake?—that far off?"

"No, no!—a monster—a huge, fierce beast!"

"Beast?" echoed Blake, grasping his bow and arrows. "Where is he? Maybe only one of these African buffaloes. How'd he look?— horns?"

"I–I didn't see any. It was all shaggy, and yellow like the grass, and terrible eyes—*Oh!*"

The girl's scream was met by a ferocious, snarling roar, so deep and prolonged that the air quivered and the very ground seemed to shake.

"God!—a lion!" cried Blake, the hair on his bare head bristling like a startled animal's.

He turned squarely about toward the ridge, his bow half drawn. Had the lion shown himself then, Blake would have shot on the instant. As it was, the beast remained behind the screening border of grass, where he could watch his intended quarry without being seen in turn. The delay gave Blake time for reflection. He spoke sharply, as it were biting off his words: "Hit out. I'll stop the bluffer."

"I can't. Oh, I'm afraid!"

Again the hidden beast gave voice to his mighty rumbling challenge. Still he did not appear, and Blake attempted a derisive jeer: "Hey, there, louder! We've not run yet! It's all right, little woman. The skulking sneak is trying to bluff us. 'Fraid to come out if we don't stampede. He'll make off when he finds we don't scare. Lions never tackle men in the daytime. Just keep cool a while. He'll—"

"Look!—there to the right!—I saw him again! He's creeping around! See the grass move!"

"That's only the wind. It eddies down—God! he is stalking around. Trying to take us from behind—curse him! He may get me, but I'll get him too,—the dirty sneak!"

The blood had flowed back into Blake's face, and showed on each cheek in a little red patch. His broad chest rose and fell slowly to deep respirations; his eyes glowed like balls of white-hot steel. He drew his bow a little tauter, and wheeled slowly to keep the arrow pointed at the slight wave in the grass which marked the stealthy movements of the lion. Miss Leslie, more terrified with every added moment of suspense, cringed around, that she might keep him between her and the hidden beast.

Minute after minute dragged by. Only a man of Blake's obstinate, sullen temperament could have withstood the strain and kept cool. Even he found the impulse to leap up and run all but irresistible. Miss Leslie crouched behind him, no more able to run than a mouse with which a cat has been playing.

Once they caught a glimpse of the sinuous, tawny form gliding among the leafless stems of a thorn clump. Blake took quick aim; but the outlines of the beast were indistinct and the range long. He hesitated, and the opportunity was lost.

Yard by yard they watched the slight swaying of the grass tops which betrayed the cautious advance of the grim stalker. The beast did not roar again. Having failed to flush his game, he was seeking to catch them off their guard, or perhaps was warily taking stock of the strange creatures, whose like he had never seen.

Now and then there was a pause, and the grass tops swayed only to the down-puffs of the heightening gale. At such moments the two grew rigid, watching and waiting in breathless suspense. They could see, as distinctly as though there had been no screening grass, the baleful eyes of the huge cat and the shaggy forebody as the beast stood still and glared out at them.

Then the sinuous wave would start on again around the grass border, and Blake would draw in a deep breath and mutter a word of encouragement to the girl: "Look, now—the dirty sneak! Trying to give us the creeps, is he? I'll creeps him! 'Fraid to show his pretty mug!"

Not until the beast had circled half around the glade did his purpose flash upon Blake. With the wariness of all savage hunters, the animal had marked out the spur of jungle on the north side, where he could creep closer to his quarry before leaping from cover.

"The damned sneak!" growled Blake. "You there, Jenny?"

She could not speak, but he heard her gasp.

"Brace up, little woman! Where's your grit? You're out of this deal, anyway. He'll choke to death swallowing me— But say; couldn't you manage to shin up a palm, twenty feet or so, and hang on for a couple of minutes I"

"I—can't move—I am—"

"Make a try! It'll give me a run for my money. I'll take the next elevator after you. That'll bring the bluffer out on the hot-foot. I slip a surprise between his ribs, and we view the scenery while he's passing in his checks. Come; make a spurt! He's around the turn, and getting nearer every step."

"I can't—Tom,—there is no need that both of us— You climb up—"

He turned about as the meaning of her whisper dawned upon him. Her eyes were shining with the ecstasy of self-sacrifice. It was only the glance of an instant; then he was again facing the jungle.

"God! You think I'd do that!"

She made no reply. There was a pause. Blake—crouched on one knee, tense and alert—waited until the sinister wave was advancing into the point of the incurved jungle. Then he spoke, in a low, even tone: "Feel if my glass is there."

Her hand reached around and pressed against the fob pocket which he had sewn in the belt of his skin trousers.

"Right. Now slip my club up under my elbow—big end. Lick on the nose'll stop a dog or a bull. It's a chance."

She thrust the club under his right elbow, and he gripped it against his side.

At that moment the lion bounded from cover, with a roar like a clap of thunder. Blake sprang erect. The beast checked himself in the act of leaping, and crouched with his great paws outstretched, every hooked claw thrust out, ready to tear and mangle. In two or three bounds he could have leaped upon Blake and crushed him with a single stroke of his paw. As he rose to repeat his deafening roar, it seemed to Blake that he stood higher than a horse—that his mouth gaped wide as the end of a hogshead. And yet the beast stood hesitating, restrained by brute dread of the unknown. Never before had any animal that he had hunted reared up to meet his attack in this strange manner.

"Lie flat!" commanded Blake; "lie flat, and don't move! I'm going to call his bluff. Keep still till the poison gets in its work. I'll keep him busy long as I can. When it's over, hit out for home along the beach. Keep inside the barricade, and watch all you can from the cliffs. Might light a fire up there nights. There's sure to be a steamer before long—"

"Tom!" she cried, struggling to her knees,—"Tom!"

But he did not pause or look around. He was beginning to circle slowly to the left across the open ground, in a spiral curve that would bring him to the edge of the jungle within thirty yards of the lion. There was red now showing in his eyes. His hair was bristling, no

165

longer with fear, but with sheer brute fury; his lips were drawn back from the clenched teeth; his nostrils distended and quivering; his forehead wrinkled like that of an angry mastiff. His look was more ferocious than that of the snarling beast he faced. All the primeval in him was roused. He was become a man of the Cave Age. He went to meet death, his mind and body aflame with fierce lust to kill.

The lion stilled his roars, and crouched as if to spring, snarling and grinning with rage and uncertainty. His eyes, unaccustomed to the glare of the mid-day sun, blinked incessantly, though he followed the man's every movement, his snarls deepening into growls at the slightest change of attitude.

In his blind animal rage, Blake had forgotten that the purpose of his lateral advance was to place as great a distance as possible between him and the girl before the clash. Yet instinct kept him moving along his spiral course, on the chance that he might catch his foe off his guard.

Suddenly the lion half rose and stretched forward, sniffing. There was an uneasy whining note in his growls. Blake let the club slip from beneath his arm, and drew his bow until the arrow-head lay upon his thumb. His outstretched arm was rigid as a bar of steel. So tense and alert were all his nerves that he knew he could drive home both arrows, and still have time to swing his club before the beast was upon him.

A puff of wind struck against his back, and swept on to the nostrils of the lion, laden with the odor of man. The beast uttered a short, startled roar, and whirling about, leaped away into the jungle so quickly that Blake's arrow flashed past a full yard behind.

The second arrow was on the string before the first had struck the ground. But the lion had vanished in the grass. With a yell, Blake dashed on across to the nearest point of the jungle. As he ran, he drew the burning-glass from his fob, and flipped it open, ready for use. If the lion had turned behind the sheltering grass stems, he was too cowardly to charge out again. Within a minute the jungle border was a wall of roaring flame.

The grass, long since dead, and bone-dry with the days of tropical sunshine since the cyclone, flared up before the wind like gunpowder. Even against the wind the fire ate its way along the ground with fearful rapidity, trailing behind it an upwhirling vortex of smoke and flame. No living creature could have burst through that belt of fire.

A wave of fierce heat sent Blake staggering back, scorched and blistered. There was no exultance in his bearing. For the moment all thought of the lion was swallowed up in awe of his own work. He stared at the hell of leaping, roaring flames from beneath his upraised arm. To the north sparks and lighted wisps of grass driven by the gale had already fired the jungle half way to the farther ridge.

Step by step Blake drew back. His heel struck against something soft. He looked down, and saw Miss Leslie lying on the sand, white and still. She had fainted, overcome by fear or by the unendurable heat. The heat must have stupefied him as well. He stared at her, dull-eyed, wondering if she was dead. His brain cleared. He sprang over to where the flask lay beside the remnants of the lunch.

He was dashing the last drops of the tepid water in her face, when she moaned, and her eyelids began to flutter. He flung down the flask, and fell to chafing her wrist.

"Tom!" she moaned.

"Yes, Miss Jenny, I'm here. It's all right," he answered.

"Have I had a sunstroke? Is that why it seems so— I can hardly breathe—"

"It's all right, I tell you. Only a little bonfire I touched off. Guess you must have fainted, but it's all right now."

"It was silly of me to faint. But when I saw that dreadful thing leap—" She faltered, and lay shuddering. Fearful that she was about to swoon again, Blake slapped her hand between his palms with stinging force.

"You're it!" he shouted. "The joke's on you! Kitty jumped just the other way, and he won't come back in a hurry with that fire to head him off. Jump up now, and we'll do a jig on the strength of it."

She attempted a smile, and a trace of color showed in her cheeks. With an idea that action would further her recovery, he drew her to a sitting position, stepped quickly behind, and, with his hands beneath her elbows, lifted her upright. But she was still too weak and giddy to stand alone. As he released his grip, she swayed and would have fallen had he not caught her arm.

"Steady!" he admonished. "Brace up; you're all right."

"I'm—I'm just a little dizzy," she murmured, clinging to his shoulder. "It will pass in a minute. It's so silly, but I'm that way—Tom, I—I think you are the bravest man—"

"Yes, yes—but that's not the point. Leave go now, like a sensible girl. It's about time to hit the trail."

He drew himself free, and without a glance at her blushing face, began to gather up their scattered outfit. His hat lay where he had weighted it down with the cocoanut. He tossed the nut into the skin bag, and jammed the hat on his head, pulling the brim far down over his eyes. When he had fetched his club, he walked back past the girl, with his eyes averted.

"Come on," he muttered.

The scarlet in the girl's cheeks swept over her whole face in a burning wave, which ebbed slowly and left her colorless. Blake had started off without a backward glance. She gazed about with a bewildered look at the palms and the barren ridge and the fiery tidal wave of flame. Her gaze came back to Blake, and she followed him.

Within a short distance she found herself out of the sheltering lee of the ridge. The first wind gust almost overthrew her. She could never have walked against such a gale; but with the wind at her back she was buoyed up and borne along as though on wings. Her sole effort was to keep her foothold. Had it been their morning trip, she could have cried out with joy and skipped along before the gusts like a school-girl. Now she walked as soberly as the wind would permit, and took care not to lessen the distance between herself and Blake.

Mile by mile they hastened back across the plain,—on their right the blue sea of water, with its white-caps and spray; on their left the yellow sea of fire, with its dun fog of smoke.

Once only had Blake looked back to see if the girl was following. After that he swung along, with down-bent head, his gaze upon the ground. Even when he passed in under the grove and around the pool to the foot of the cleft, he began the ascent without waiting to assist her up the break in the path. The girl came after, her lips firm, her eyes bright and expectant. She drew herself up the ledge as though she had been bred to mountain climbing.

Inside the barricade Blake was waiting to close the opening. She crept through, and rose to catch him by the sleeve.

"Tom, look at me," she said. "Once I was most unjust to you in my thoughts. I wronged you. Now I must tell you that I think you are the bravest—the noblest man—"

"Get away!" he exclaimed, and he shook off her hand roughly. "Don't be a fool! You don't know what you're talking about."

"But I do, Tom. I believe that you are—"

"I'm a blackguard—do you hear?"

"No blackguard is brave. The way you faced that terrible beast—"

"Yes, blackguard—to've gone and shown to you that I—to've let you say a single word—Can't you see? Even if I'm not what you call a

168

gentleman, I thought I knew how any man ought to treat a woman—but to go and let you know, before we'd got back among people!"

"But—but, Tom, why not, if we—"

"No!" he retorted harshly. "I'm going now to pile up wood on the cliff for a beacon fire. In the morning I'll start making that catamaran—"

"No, you shall not— You shall not go off, and leave me, and—and risk your life! I can't bear to think of it! Stay with me, Tom—dear! Even if a ship never came—"

He turned resolutely, so as not to see her blushing face.

"Come now, Miss Leslie," he said in a dry, even tone; "don't make it so awfully hard. Let's be sensible, and shake hands on it, like two real comrades—"

She struck frantically at his outstretched hand.

"Keep away—I hate you!" she cried.

Before he could speak, she was running up the cleft.

CHAPTER XXV

IN DOUBLE SALVATION

When, an hour or more after dawn the next morning, the girl slowly drew open her door and came out of the cave, Blake was nowhere in sight. She sighed, vastly relieved, and hastened across to bathe her flushed face in the spring. Stopping every few moments to listen for his step down the cleft, she gathered up a hamper of food and fled to the tree-ladder.

As she drew herself up on the cliff, she noticed a thin column of smoke rising from the last smouldering brands of a beacon fire that had been built in the midst of the bird colony, on the extreme outer edge of the headland. She did not, however, observe that, while the smoke column streamed up from the fire directly skyward, beyond it there was a much larger volume of smoke, which seemed to have eddied down the cliff face and was now rolling up into view from out over the sea. She gave no heed to this, for the sight of the beacon had instantly alarmed her with the possibility that Blake was still on the headland, and would imagine that she was seeking him.

She paused, her cheeks aflame. But the only sign of Blake that she could see was the fire itself. She reflected that he might very well have left before dawn. As likely as not, he had descended at the north end of the cleft, and had gone off to the river to start his catamaran. At the thought all the color ebbed from her cheeks and left her white and trembling. Again she stood hesitating. With a sigh she started on toward the signal staff.

She was close upon the border of the bird colony, when Blake sat up from behind a ledge, and she found herself staring into his blinking eyes.

"Hello!" he mumbled drowsily. He sprang up, wide awake, and flushing with the guilty consciousness of what he had done. "Look at the sun—way up! Didn't mean to oversleep, Miss Leslie. You see I was up pretty late, tending the beacon. But of course that's no excuse—"

"Don't!" she exclaimed. There were tears in her eyes; yet she smiled as she spoke. "I know what you mean by 'pretty late.' You've been up all night."

"No, I haven't. Not all night—"

"To be sure! I quite understand, Mr. Thomas Blake!... Now, sit down, and eat this luncheon."

"Can't. Haven't time. I've got to get to the river and set to work. I'll get some jerked beef and eat it on the way. You see—"

"Tom!" she protested.

"It's for you," he rejoined, and his lips closed together resolutely.

He was stepping past her, when over the seaward edge of the cliff there came a sound like the yell of a raging sea-monster.

"Siren!" shouted Blake, whirling about.

The cloud of smoke beyond the cliff end was now rolling up more to the left. He dashed away towards the north edge of the cliff as though he intended to leap off into space. The girl ran after him as fast as she could over the loose stones. Before she had covered half the distance she saw him halt on the very brink of the cliff, and begin to wave and shout like a madman. A few steps farther on she caught sight of the steamer. It was lying close in, only a little way off the north point of the headland.

Even as she saw the vessel, its siren responded to Blake's wild gestures with a series of joyous screams. There could be no mistake. He had been seen. Already they were letting go anchor, and there was a little crowd of men gathering about one of the boats. Blake turned and started on a run for the cliff. But Miss Leslie darted before him, compelling him to halt.

"Wait!" she cried, her eyes sparkling with happy tears. "Tom, it's come now. You needn't—"

"Let me by! I'm going to meet them. I want to—"

But she put her hands upon his shoulders.

"Tom!" she whispered, "let it be now, before any one—anything can possibly come between us! Let it be a part of our life here—here, where I've learned how brave and true a real man can be!"

"And then have him prove himself a sneak!" he cried. "No; I won't, Jenny! I've got you to think of. Wait till I've seen your father. Ten to one, he'll not hear of it—he'll cut you off without a cent. Not but what I'd be glad myself; but you're used to luxuries, girlie, and I'm a poor man. I can't give them to you—"

She laid a hand on his mouth, and smiled up at him in tender mockery.

"Come, now, Mr. Blake; you're not very complimentary. After surviving my cooking all these weeks, don't you think I might do, at a pinch, for a poor man's wife!"

"No, Jenny!" he protested, trying to draw back. "You oughtn't to decide now. When you get back among your friends, things may look different. Think of your society friends! Wait till you see me with other men—gentlemen! I'm just a rough, uncultured, ordinary—"

"Hush!" she cried, and she again placed her hand on his mouth. "You sha'n't say such cruel things about Tom—my Tom—the man I trust—that I—"

Her arms slipped about his neck, and her eyes shone up into his with tender radiance.

"Don't!" he begged hoarsely. "'T ain't fair! I—I can't stand it!"

"The man I love!" she whispered.

He crushed her to him in his great arms.

"My little girl!—dear little girl!" he repeated, and he pressed his lips to her hair.

She snuggled her face closer against his shoulder, and replied in a very small voice, "I—I suppose you know that ship captains can m-marry people."

"But I haven't even a job yet!" he exclaimed. "Suppose your father—"

"Please listen!" she pleaded. There was a sound like suppressed sobbing.

"What is it?" he ventured, and he listened, greatly perturbed. The muffled voice sounded very meek and plaintive: "I'll try to do my part, Mr. Blake,—really I will! I—I hope we can manage to struggle along—somehow. You know, I have a little of my own. It's only three—three million; but—"

"What!" he demanded, and he held her out at arm's length, to stare at her in frowning bewilderment. "If I'd known that, I'd—"

"You'd never have given me a chance to—to propose to you, you dear old silly!" she cried, her eyes dancing with tender mirth. "See here!"

She turned from him, and back again, and held up a withered, crumpled flower. He looked, and saw that it was the amaryllis blossom.

"You—kept it!"

"Because—because, even then, down in the bottom of my heart, I had begun to realize—to know what you were like—and of course that meant— Tom, tell me! Do you think I'm utterly shameless? Do you blame me for being the one to—to—"

"Blame you!" he cried. He paused to put a finger under her chin and raise her down-bent face. His eyes were very blue, but there was a twinkle in their depths. "Oh, yes; it was dreadful, wasn't it? But I guess I've no complaint to file just now."

www.ingramcontent.com/pod-product-compliance
Lightning Source LLC
Chambersburg PA
CBHW060418260626
47161CB00005B/1678